An Autobiography of a BHIKHARI

By Deepak Obhan

Clever Fox® PUBLISHING
Chennai • Bangalore

CLEVER FOX PUBLISHING
Chennai, India

Published by CLEVER FOX PUBLISHING 2025

ISBN: 978-93-3434-366-3

Written by Deepak Obhan

Disclaimer

An Autobiography of a Bhikhari is a work of autobiographical fiction. Though it draws inspiration from real-life struggles, emotional truths and societal realities, the characters, incidents, dialogues and settings portrayed in this book are products of the author's imagination or used fictitiously. Any resemblance to actual persons, living or deceased, or to real events or places is purely coincidental and unintentional.

This novel presents a deeply emotional journey of a soul who falls from privilege into poverty—not to seek pity, but to awaken empathy. The narrative explores themes such as abandonment, suffering, injustice, identity, resilience and hope. It may evoke strong feelings or stir personal reflections in readers, especially those who have lived through hardship or marginalization.

The intention of this book is not to defame, discredit or hurt any individual, caste, creed, religion, institution or social class. Rather, it is to shine a light on the invisible lives that often go unnoticed and to give a voice to those silenced by circumstance.

Readers are encouraged to approach the story with an open heart and mind. Interpretations drawn from this work are subjective and the author shall not be held liable for any misrepresentation or emotional impact beyond the purpose of storytelling and awareness.

This novel is dedicated to the unheard, the forgotten and the misunderstood. May their stories not remain buried beneath dust and indifference.

Authors Note

Writing *An Autobiography of a Bhikhari* has been more than just a creative process—it has been a spiritual and emotional journey. This story is born not only from imagination, but also from observation, empathy and silent conversations with the world around. It is a voice for the voiceless, a mirror for the forgotten and a hand stretched out from the shadows of society.

The character of Deepak is not just one boy. He is many. He is every child who has slept hungry, every youth who has questioned his worth and every soul who has been judged by the dirt on his clothes instead of the depth of his heart. He represents those who once had everything and ended up with nothing… and yet carried on.

This 50 Chapters book is not about glorifying suffering or romanticizing poverty. It is about understanding what it means to lose, to break, to beg—not only for food, but for love, dignity and identity. It is about resilience and the silent strength that grows in the hearts of those who are abandoned by fate.

Some parts of this story are deeply emotional. Others are stitched together from the lives of people I've passed by, read about or simply imagined—wondering what their world must feel like. If this book makes you pause, reflect or feel something stir within you, then its purpose is fulfilled.

Thank you for choosing to walk this path with Deepak. May his story live on in your heart.

With gratitude and hope,

Deepak Obhan

Written by Deepak Obhan

Written by Deepak Obhan

Chapter 1 : My Birth

Destiny had already carved my path to become a *Bhikhari* (beggar), even though I was born into privilege — with a golden spoon in my mouth, under the soft glow of a chandelier in a plush private hospital in Delhi. The irony of life, perhaps, begins at birth — and mine was no exception.

My parents, both respected doctors with flourishing careers, had waited seven long years for my arrival. I was their miracle, their only child, their answered prayer after years of medical hope and silent heartbreak.

The day I was born, the entire family erupted in joy as though a festival had been declared. Sweets were distributed to neighbours, relatives flew in from across the country. No one could have guessed that the child who arrived with such celebration would one day be forgotten by the same world that cheered for him.

The first person to hold me wasn't my mother or father — it was a doctor. I still remember, as if it were etched into the fibers of my soul, being lifted from the warm comfort of my mother's womb and thrust into the blinding lights of the delivery room. The doctor held me with professional ease, turned me upside down and patted my bare bottom. I was stunned — was I being punished already? Only later did I realize that he wasn't toying with me; he was coaxing my first cry — the sound that would signal life. When I finally wailed, he smiled with satisfaction and said, "Congratulations, it's a boy!"

Next came the Aaya Bai — a woman with firm hands but a kind face. She bathed me in lukewarm water, her touch efficient yet surprisingly gentle. She wrapped me so tightly in a white cloth that only my face was left visible — like a tiny soldier, all swaddled and ready for battle. I looked like a chicken roll; rapped from all the sides, where only my face was visible and my limbs immobilized in that strange fabric cocoon.

Everything around me appeared in shades of green — the nurses' uniforms, the surgical curtains, the walls. It felt like I had been born into a garden of uniforms.

Then, they handed me to a woman whose eyes were heavy with fatigue and yet glowed with something I couldn't name at the time. She was drenched in sweat as if she just came down from the treadmill, her hospital gown clinging to her like a second skin, her breath shallow but steady. She took me in her arms and kissed my forehead with a trembling intensity I would later recognize as maternal love. That woman was my mother — the one who bore pain and hope in equal measure to bring me into this world.

And then came a man — tall, anxious and visibly shaken. His hands trembled as he reached out for me, as if afraid I might shatter. His eyes were wet but not from pain — they overflowed with wonder, disbelief and an overwhelming tenderness. He cradled me carefully, as though I were made of glass and his lips quivered as he whispered, "Beta, I am your father." That was the moment I felt something I couldn't describe — a kind of warmth, a strange familiarity, an unspoken promise. I didn't know his name, but I knew he would protect me. At least, that's what I believed then.

The days that followed were a parade of faces, voices and fragrances. Nearly a hundred relatives came to see me — flooding the hospital and later our home with laughter, noise and endless blessings. Some brought toys, others cash or gold trinkets. A few came just to take photos or sip tea. They called me everything sweet and royal — *Ladla*, *Rajkumar*, *Sona*, *Sweety*, *Cutiepie*... Names filled with love, dreams and expectations. But none called me *Bhikhari*. No one saw it coming.

No one — not even the stars — hinted at the life that awaited me. A life far from the silk sheets I was born into. A life on the streets, under the open sky, where food was uncertain and love was a distant luxury.

But for now, I was the prince of the moment — the celebrated newborn. And like all stories that start with light, mine too was destined to travel through darkness.

Chapter 2 : The Day I Was Parcelled Home

The day I was discharged from Sanjeevani Hospital was supposed to be the beginning of a beautiful life — the first step out into the world from the safe, sterile walls of the maternity ward. My parents had planned everything meticulously. I was dressed in a tiny denim jumpsuit, soft as clouds, with little yellow buttons shaped like ducks. My mother had placed me gently in a colourful, imported rocking chair — more throne than carrier — with soft cushions embroidered with stars and moons.

Everything about the moment looked perfect from the outside. A new family, a new journey, a new life.

As the nurse wheeled my mother towards the car, a slight tremble crossed her face. She tried to smile but failed. Just as she reached the car's open door, her knees buckled and she collapsed, unconscious, at the threshold of a dream she had waited seven years for. The smile on my father's face disappeared instantly. Panic seized him. He jumped out of the driver's seat, yelling, "Help! Help!" as though the word alone could heal her.

A crowd quickly gathered. Hospital staff rushed to assist. Some passersby tried to lift my mother, others simply stood by — whispering, pointing, unsure whether to intervene or just watch the drama unfold like spectators at a play.

In all the chaos, one detail went unnoticed: the car door had been left wide open… and I was still inside.

It was in that forgotten moment — lost between concern and confusion — that a man stepped forward. He looked ordinary. Maybe a little too ordinary. Nobody paid him much attention. Without a word, he walked up to the car, reached inside and picked me up as if I belonged to him. I didn't cry. I didn't scream. I didn't know I was being taken away — I had no reason to doubt anyone yet. In my infant mind, every face was still unfamiliar and every touch, still new. I thought maybe he was an uncle, a family friend, another relative come to help.

But we didn't return to the hospital.

We didn't return to my father.

We didn't return to my mother, still lying unconscious on the ground.
Instead, we boarded a taxi — then another — and then one more. Each one took us further and further away from the only world I had known for a few days. By the third taxi, even in my baby brain, something shifted. The man's silence felt heavier. The world outside the window no longer looked familiar. I wasn't being taken home. I was being *taken.*

Finally, after what seemed like hours, we reached a small, cramped house tucked inside a labyrinth of narrow lanes and rusted tin roofs. The smell of damp walls and kerosene filled the air. Inside, ten children of varying ages played, fought and moved about like clockwork — some were quiet, some loud, all barefoot. Their clothes were torn, their hands grimy, their voices rough — but their eyes… their eyes were kind. Curious. Warm.

I was the youngest. The new recruit!

The older kids rushed to see me. Two of them — a boy of eleven and a girl of about nine — took charge like miniature parents. They gently changed my clothes, wiped me down with a cloth soaked in lukewarm water and fed me what they called *dudu*. It was milk — but not like the one my mother had stored in glass bottles for me. This was thinner, strange-tasting and warm in a different way. Still, I drank it. Hunger doesn't come with choices.

As I slowly began to take in the unfamiliar faces and voices around me, the door creaked open again.

In walked a woman — tall, with sharp features and a cold expression. She wore a synthetic saree and heavy gold-colored bangles that clinked with every step. Her name was Laxmi Aunty. She didn't ask any questions. She didn't smile. She examined me like one would inspect a piece of furniture at a bazaar. Then, she opened her purse and handed the man fifty thousand rupees in cash. No words, no paperwork. Just an exchange. Like I was a parcel — fragile, but replaceable.

And just like that, I was sold.

Laxmi Aunty bundled me up and boarded the next train from Nizamuddin Station — headed west, toward Mumbai. I had never seen a train before. Its noise terrified me, but I was too tired, too drugged, to cry. She gave me milk laced with something that dulled my senses and pulled me into a deep, dreamless sleep. That was my first experience of what I would later call *sleeping dudu*. A trick to keep babies silent on long journeys to strange futures.

As the train thundered along the tracks, I drifted in and out of sleep. The rhythmic rocking reminded me of my fancy chair — the one I had left behind in my parents' car. The gentle sway, the muffled sounds of stations passing by and the strange warmth of Laxmi Aunty's lap — they became my new lullaby.

By the time we reached Bandra Station 24 hours later, my name, my fate and my future had all changed. I had arrived in Mumbai not as the beloved son of two doctors, but as someone else's commodity.

A baby, parcelled across cities.

A soul, sold before it could even speak.

A destiny rewritten… without my consent.

Chapter 3 : A New Life in Dharavi

After the long, jarring train ride that felt like an eternity, we reached the city's belly — not its heart, but a place hidden behind layers of survival and sorrow. From the station, we took an auto-rickshaw through narrow lanes choked with noise, dust and humanity. Eventually, we stopped at a place that looked nothing like a home — Dharavi, Asia's largest slum. It was a maze of tin roofs, broken walls and crooked alleys. And somehow, in that chaos, I was supposed to start over. That was home now.

Laxmi Aunty's "house" was a single room with no windows, barely enough space to stretch out. She lived there with three children who would soon become my new family — Ayush, the clever and watchful seven-year-old; Bhumi, gentle and always humming something eight-year-old; and Agni, the youngest, full of untamed energy five-year-old. They weren't my blood, but they became my siblings in survival.

The next morning, something strange happened. Another woman came and took me away. She was kind at first, but before long, she offered me what they all seemed to have — a bottle filled with "sleeping dudu." It tasted strange, sweet and heavy. I drank it because I was told to. I drank it because I was tired, scared and numb. This became my new routine. Every day, a new face. Every day, more sleeping dudu. I didn't know what it was. All I knew was that it made everything blur and helped me forget — until my body started breaking.

After a month, the constant sedation took its toll. I stopped eating, my limbs turned heavy, my head burned with fever. One night, I collapsed. In panic, Laxmi Aunty rushed me to a doctor. But he wasn't the saviour I imagined. He was harsh, angry. He yelled at her — words I couldn't understand but felt like thunder. And then he jabbed a needle into my bottom without warning. I screamed so loudly, I thought my voice would crack. But strangely, it worked. My fever began to subside and slowly, my head cleared.

In those painful days, Ayush and Bhumi became my protectors. Though they were children themselves, they showed a wisdom beyond their years. Somehow, they always managed to sneak me clean water or a little plain dudu that didn't make me sleepy. They would press cold cloths to my forehead and tell me stories until I fell asleep. I don't know how, but they made me feel human again.

Laxmi Aunty, on the other hand, didn't seem to care much about cleanliness or comfort. Bathing was a luxury we couldn't afford — it happened once, maybe twice a month, usually only when the smell became unbearable. Clothes were handed down from child to child, old and torn, rarely washed. But even in that neglect, there were moments of unexpected happiness. On Diwali, she'd bring home bags of "new" clothes — actually discards from rich people's homes. They still smelled of soap and perfume and to us, they felt like silk. I remember hugging a red sweater once, my nose buried in it, thinking it smelled like heaven.

Life in Dharavi was not kind. But it was real. And somehow, through the dirt, pain and hunger, small glimmers of hope kept us going. Ayush's jokes, Bhumi's lullabies, Agni's laughter and the occasional whiff of perfumed fabric — those were the lights in my dark tunnel.

Chapter 4 : The Festival That Gave Me a Name

My first Diwali in Dharavi was not one of joy, but of fear.

The night sky burst into flames of color, but all I could hear were explosions — sharp, violent, terrifying. Each cracker that burst outside felt like a war being fought right outside our door. I cried for hours, clutching at my ears, trembling as the room vibrated with the sound of celebration I didn't yet understand.

Ayush, ever thoughtful, tried to help. He rolled little bits of cotton — the same ones we used to light diyas — and gently pushed them into my ears. His hands were warm, his voice calming, but the sound still broke through. My sobs didn't stop that night. That Diwali was not light for me. It was noise, confusion and shadows.

But time does something to the soul. It teaches it how to bend without breaking.

By the next Diwali, I had learned the rhythm of the slum — the daily thunder of trains, the shouts from the marketplace, the endless barking of stray dogs. The sound of crackers still startled me, but I no longer cried. And more importantly, that year, I could walk.

It happened a few days before Diwali. My legs had been growing stronger and I had been wobbling from wall to wall for weeks. Then one morning, as golden light streamed through the cracks in our tin roof, I let go of the wall — and took a step.

Just one step.

Then another.

Ayush saw me first. His eyes widened with joy and pride as if he'd just witnessed magic.

"Aunty! Aunty!" he screamed, running out like he'd seen a miracle.

Bhumi and Agni joined in, clapping and shouting. The room filled with a kind of electricity I hadn't felt before.

Laxmi Aunty was outside, squatting on a low stool, chopping vegetables on an old steel plate. When she heard the children's screams, she dropped everything and rushed in, her hands still wet with turmeric and onion juice.

Her eyes locked onto me, standing — trembling, uncertain, but upright. And in that moment, the expression on her face changed. It softened. It brightened. She didn't say anything for a long time.

Then she whispered, as if to herself, "He's walking... on Diwali." She crouched down beside me, touched my cheek and said, "You are our Deepak — our lamp of hope."

And just like that, I had a name.

Deepak.

In Hindu tradition, *Deepak* means lamp — a symbol of light, of warmth, of triumph over darkness.

That Diwali, the festival of lights gave me more than hand-me-down clothes and leftover sweets. It gave me an identity.

To mark the occasion, Aunty cooked something special — a rare luxury. Rice with ghee, jaggery and a few cashews. We didn't have enough plates, so we sat cross-legged on the floor, eating from steel lids and bowls. The food was simple, but that night it tasted like a feast.

We laughed, we lit diyas and for the first time, I felt like I belonged.

That was the beginning.

From a mansion in South Delhi to the slums of Dharavi.

From silver spoons to tin plates.

From a name forgotten to a name reborn.

That's how I came into this new world.

That's how I was named.

And that's how I began my journey

— **from a millionaire's son…**

to a Bhikhari.

Chapter 5 : My First Earning

After the incident at the hospital, something changed. Laxmi Aunty stopped sending me out with the other aunties. I think I was around three years old when she finally decided I was ready to join my siblings at the traffic signals. It was time, she thought, for me to *learn begging*—as if it were a skill one could master like reading or writing.

Each day, one of my siblings would take turns holding me while standing at various traffic junctions, waiting for the red light to halt the stream of cars. That was our window. That was when we *worked.*

Ayush later told me about my first day. A sleek, shiny car stopped in front of us. The tinted window rolled down slowly and from inside, a beautiful lady called out softly—"Ssshh... Ssshh…" as if she was calling a stray cat. She then asked Ayush, "What's his name?" He proudly replied, "Madam, Deepak."

She looked at me, smiled warmly and without saying another word, handed me a crisp ₹500 note. Just like that. That was the first money I ever earned.

Laxmi Aunt's eyes lit up when she saw the note. She was overjoyed, but I couldn't understand why that happiness felt so cruel. Within moments, celebration turned to punishment.

She dragged me to the kitchen, placed dry red chilies on a hot iron pan over the *chulha* and then held my face close to the rising smoke. I coughed and gasped, my eyes burned, my throat felt like fire. I didn't understand what was happening. For a moment, I wondered, *Is she cooking pizza and mistook me for oregano?*

My face turned red, like an Angry Bird and soon enough, I burst into tears. That's when Bhumi came to the rescue. She gently took me in her arms and started playing with me until I calmed down.

Only much later did I realize it wasn't punishment—it was ritual. Aunty believed I had attracted the evil eye because of the unusually large amount I earned. That chili smoke was her way of "cleansing" me.

That night was a celebration. Aunty made chicken curry from the money I had brought in. It was a feast—something rare in our little world. We all sat together and shared the meal, our hearts and bellies full for once.

Ayush, ever the sentimental one, wanted to preserve a memory of my first earning. We couldn't afford to save the ₹500 note—money like that doesn't stay long in hands like ours. So, he cleaned one of the chicken bones from dinner and threaded it with a piece of black string. He tied it around my neck, like a pendant. That bone became my first keepsake—a symbol of survival, of contribution, of *belonging*.

From the next day onward, I was on duty full-time. Morning to evening, we stood at different signals, hands outstretched, eyes hopeful. Our income nearly doubled. Aunty noticed. She began treating me with a little more care—not out of love, but because I had become an *asset*. If I fell sick, the income would dip. I was no longer just a child—I was a source of revenue.

Begging became routine. Eventually, I even performed solo. My charm, my luck—whatever it was—worked. Our earnings grew. We had enough food to eat every day and even some left to save for the days when the traffic lights wouldn't be kind.

And that's the memory of my first earning—immortalized not in currency, but in the form of a chicken bone strung around my neck. A token of a day that changed the course of my life.

Chapter 6 : Festivals in India

India is known worldwide for its vibrant culture and countless festivals, celebrated across various religions and communities. From an early age, I was introduced to this colourful world—not from the comfort of a home, but from the streets, where festivals had a different meaning for us. It weren't just about a rituals or joy—it meant more people, more emotion and more chances to earn.

Laxmi Aunty would plan ahead for every upcoming festival. She would buy items for us to wear or sell—matching the season, the traditions and most importantly, the crowd. Each month brought new clothes, new goods and new hope.

The first festival I witnessed after my initial earning was **Christmas**. We wore red Santa Claus caps and sold them along with sparkly hairbands at traffic signals. We even changed our regular spots and moved near churches and Christian communities. Our sales soared through the season, lasting till New Year. I remember seeing a real-life Santa—jolly, plump, with a fluffy white beard—handing out chocolates to kids. To my surprise, I got one too. On New Year's Eve, people partied late into the night. We begged outside the venues, earning much more than usual.

Next came **Makar Sankranti**, when the skies filled with colourful kites. So, we started selling kites too. This usually started some 3-4 weeks before the main festival and last even some more days after the festival. This time, we shifted to predominantly Maharashtrian & Gujarati neighbourhoods. People were generous, offering us *til-gul*—a traditional sweet shared during this festival. While children laughed and cheered watching their kites fly, I noticed birds falling from the sky, injured by the razor-sharp strings. It did hurt to see, but I had no choice. My survival depended on selling those very kites. The more we sell kits the more we get money.

As **Republic Day** approached, we sold the Indian flag. This day marks the adoption of our Constitution in 1950, drafted by Dr. B.R. Ambedkar. There was a sense of unity—everyone, regardless of caste or religion, celebrated it. We returned to our original streets and did well. But my joy turned to confusion the next day when I saw those same flags, once held with pride, lying abandoned on the streets—left to be cleaned up by street sweepers.

Soon after, **Valentine's Day** arrived—not a traditional festival, but a celebration embraced by all, especially the youth. We sold red roses near colleges and public gardens. I always found it strange—people bought these expensive roses for their lovers, but often forgot to show that same love to those who truly cared for them, like their parents. On this one day, a single rose could sell for ten times its normal price.

The next festival was **Maha Shivratri**, dedicated to Lord Shiva. We begged near temples as devotees lined up to pour milk on the Shiva Lingam. I stood near the temple's drainage outlet, collecting the milk from the drainage pipe by filtering it through a handkerchief. For someone who rarely tasted milk, it felt like luxury. I even skipped my meal that day—I had more milk than I'd ever had in my life. I wondered why people couldn't worship like this every day, so I could drink milk more often.

Then came the **festival of colours—Holi**. We sold powdered colours and plastic bags used for water balloons. Kids would gleefully throw water-filled balloons at unsuspecting strangers—especially women and those on bikes. On Holi, everyone turned into walking rainbows. Some people drank *bhang*, made from cannabis and acted silly, laughing endlessly. I remember Laxmi Aunty tried it once—she laughed all day like a child. I had never seen her so happy. But the next day, I saw animals, especially cows, falling sick after eating the plastic waste left behind.

Gudi Padwa, the Maharashtrian New Year, was next. We moved to areas with a higher Maharashtrian population. Streets were decorated with rangoli and *Gudis*—flags adorned with flowers, neem leaves and silver pots—stood tall outside homes. People shared traditional meals with us, giving us a taste of celebration.

Then came a double celebration: **Baisakhi** and **Dr. Ambedkar Jayanti**. In the morning, we begged outside Gurudwaras, where the Sikh community celebrated their New Year. Later, we were invited in for *langar*—a free meal served to all. In the evening, our neighbourhood lit up with music and speeches as we celebrated Dr. Ambedkar's birthday. That day, we had delicious meals twice and it felt like a feast meant for kings.

After this, there was a gap in festivals for a while and we returned to our usual signals. Those days were usually hot summers, I guess it's because of the heat that people don't want to celebrate any festivals.

When **Friendship Day** arrived, we sold colourful friendship bands. School and college students, as well as working professionals, tied these bands on the wrists of their friends. The crowd was diverse and so were the earnings.

Soon after, **Independence Day** came. Once again, we sold flags and returned to patriotic streets. People of all backgrounds came together. There were flag hoisting ceremonies in neighbourhoods, schools and offices. But, as with Republic Day, the flags were tossed aside the very next morning. I often wondered—why can't people preserve a flag with the same care they give their clothes, jewellery or money?

Raksha Bandhan followed—a day to celebrate the bond between brothers and sisters. We sold *rakhis* on the streets and at home, Bhumi and Agni tied rakhis on our wrists. Laxmi Aunty cooked a special meal and we stayed home that day. For once, we played like normal children.

Then came **Eid**, celebrated by the Muslim community. They fasted for an entire month before the festival. We begged near mosques and were often offered fruits and fried treats during the evenings. On Eid, Laxmi Aunty cooked mutton at home—a rare treat for us.

As **Janmashtami** approached, we returned to temples. Lord Krishna's birth was celebrated with devotion. We begged until midnight and the next day participated in *Dahi Handi* celebrations—where human pyramids are formed to break a hanging pot of curd. Being the youngest, I was always the one climbing to the top.

Then came the grandeur of **Ganesh Chaturthi**—eleven days of devotion, joy and music. Pandals were set up everywhere and we begged outside them, blending with the crowds. When the festival ended, idols of Lord Ganesha were immersed in water, leaving behind memories and sometimes, a lot of waste.

After the gods, it was time to remember the **Father of the Nation—Mahatma Gandhi**. His birthday, October 2nd, was a national holiday. Families went out for picnics or mall outings and we followed them, hoping for a kind hand.

Next was **Dussehra**, symbolizing the victory of good over evil. We begged outside Durga Pandals, watching performances of Ramayana and the burning of Ravana effigies. It was a Nine-day celebration of colours, prayers and hope.

And then came the biggest of all—**Diwali**. The festival of lights. We sold handmade *diyas* on the streets and begged outside jewellery shops, malls, parks and movie theatres. People shopped, dined and lit up their homes with joy. At home, we did our small puja and Laxmi Aunty gave us sweets. Crackers lit up the skies—and polluted the air.

On the last day, **Bhai Dooj** was celebrated—similar to Raksha Bandhan. We often received old clothes in donation and that alone made us feel special.

Year after year, the same cycle continued. We begged through festivals, grew through them and understood India through them. With so many religions and cultures, we had multiple opportunities to earn—and to survive.

Every festival taught us something, but one thing remained true—beneath all differences, everyone is human. And sometimes, from that human heart, came kindness… in the form of a coin, a meal or a smile.

Chapter 7 : Seasonal Begging

Begging isn't just about asking—it's about enduring. Every season brings its own challenges and each one tests not only your body, but also your spirit. While others look forward to the change in weather, for us, it meant adapting our way of surviving—reshaping how, where and even *if* we could beg.

Begging in Summers

Summer on the streets was brutal. The heat would blaze down like a curse from the sky. Our skins would burn, our heads would ache and the streets—usually crowded—would empty out during the hottest hours. The tar on the roads would become so hot that it could literally burn your feet if you stood too long without slippers. Most of us, including me, didn't have proper footwear.

Begging during summer meant standing at traffic signals under the scorching sun, wiping sweat off our faces every few seconds. The worst part was the dehydration. We didn't have access to cold water or shade and at times, even finding drinking water felt like a mission. We'd wait outside shops or offices, hoping someone would spare a bottle or let us use a tap. Sometimes, we would drink from leaking pipes or taps in public toilets just to survive.

But summer had one hidden benefit—people felt guilty seeing us suffer in the heat. A few kind souls would offer us cold drinks, water bottles or fruits. Some would lower their car windows and hand out ice cream to kids. For those brief moments, we felt seen—not just as beggars, but as fellow humans.

Clothing became a struggle too. We couldn't afford light, breathable fabrics. We wore whatever we had, often old, faded, synthetic clothes that trapped the heat. At night, sleeping on the footpath was worse—the heat radiated from the cement and there was no breeze. We slept in sweat, sticking to each other like glue, unable to breathe freely.

Summer taught us the art of waiting—waiting for shade, waiting for kindness, waiting for the sun to go down so we could breathe again.

Begging in Monsoons

If summer burned us, the **monsoon** drowned us.

Rain, for most people, brings joy. Children splash in puddles, lovers dance under the sky and families gather near windows sipping hot tea. But for us, the rain meant soaked clothes, wet floors, damp food and the constant fear of falling sick.

Plastic sheets became our only protection. Laxmi Aunty would try to gather old tarpaulin or polythene sheets and tie them around our makeshift shelter with wires, ropes or anything she could find. But no matter how hard we tried; rainwater always found a way in.

Begging during monsoon was almost impossible on some days. Signals would be flooded, traffic would slow down and people were too busy trying to protect themselves to notice a kid in wet clothes knocking at their window. We'd be drenched all day, shivering, waiting for someone to care.

Our stock—whatever we tried to sell—would get ruined. Flowers or bands, nothing stayed dry unless we somehow managed to keep them in sealed bags, which again, cost money we didn't have.

Monsoon was also the season of sickness. Fever, cold, infections—they would sweep through our group like wildfire. Without medicine or proper food, even a minor illness felt deadly. The kids cried more. The elders coughed more. And at night, we'd try to sleep in wet clothes, under a leaky sheet, praying the rain would stop for just one night.

But amidst the chaos, monsoon had rare moments of kindness. A few strangers would hand us raincoats, umbrellas or warm soup. And every time it happened; it felt like a miracle.

Begging in Winters

Winter on the streets was a silent torture.

Unlike summer or monsoon, winter didn't shout—it whispered. It crept in slowly, wrapping the nights in a biting chill that made your bones ache. We'd huddle together like kittens, sharing whatever warmth our bodies could provide. Although winter was very small in Mumbai and last for few weeks only.

Warm clothes were rare treasures. Old donated sweaters, torn shawls, mismatched socks—anything that provided even the slightest insulation was used. Sometimes, we'd light small fires on the roadside using dry leaves and trash, trying to warm our hands before going to sleep. A few of us—especially the elderly and children like me—would fall terribly sick during this season because we get wet while begging on the streets.

Winter taught us resilience. It taught us to hold each other tighter, to keep moving even when your limbs didn't want to and to find hope in the warmth of one donated sweater or a stranger's cup of tea.

Each season came and went, but we stayed. We changed with them—our routines, our hopes, our hustle. Whether under the blazing sun, relentless rain or biting cold, we begged. Not just for money, but for survival, for warmth, for recognition.

Seasonal begging wasn't just about weather. It was about adaptation. It was a constant reminder that while the world turned its calendar with joy, we turned ours with fear... wondering what the next season would take from us—and what little it might give.

Chapter 8 : The People on the Streets

The streets which were my school, my playground, my battlefield—and the people on them, my teachers. Each person I met, whether they were rich or poor, kind or cruel, stranger or familiar, shaped my journey in some way. Some taught me survival. Some taught me pain. And some, unknowingly, taught me hope.

Fellow Beggars: My Street Family

We were a scattered tribe, connected by poverty and pain. Though we came from different cities, religions and stories, the streets tied us together. There were elderly beggars with deep wrinkles and tired eyes who had spent decades on the footpath. Some were disabled, some abandoned and some simply unlucky.

Bhumi, Agni and Ayush the others in my group were my siblings not by blood, but by bond. We fought for food, played with garbage, laughed at nothing and slept tangled like puppies on a cold night. Every day with them was a lesson in endurance and every night was a promise to look out for each other again tomorrow.

Street Vendors: The Survivors

Next to our begging spots were the vendors—the sellers of balloons, toys, chips, flowers and dreams. They were slightly better off than us, but only just. We shared space, water and sometimes even leftover food. Some vendors were kind, giving us old stock to sell and keep the profits. Others were hostile, calling us names and driving us away, afraid we'd scare their customers.

But one thing was clear—they hustled just like us. Their lives, too, were uncertain, shaped by police raids, bad sales and the weather.

The Police: Fear in Uniform

For us, the sound of a police whistle was a warning. We didn't see law and order—we saw lathis, threats and shouts. Some officers were kind enough to ignore us or warn us gently to move. But most treated us like trash, pushing us away from public places, destroying our makeshift shelters and sometimes even slapping us for being in the wrong place at the wrong time.

I still remember once when an officer picked up our entire food stash and threw it in the drain because we were sitting too close to a mall entrance. That day, hunger stung worse than usual.

The Rich: Behind Glass Windows

The people in big cars always fascinated me. Shiny, clean and mostly silent—they were in another world, just inches away, yet unreachable. Some rolled down their windows to give coins or left over food. Some avoided eye contact, pretending we didn't exist. And some took photos with us—for social media, not for help.

I used to wonder: why did some people have everything and still not smile, while we had nothing and still laughed over a half-rotten banana?

The Kind Strangers

There were angels in disguise—people who made a small moment feel like a miracle. I remember a young girl once tied a friendship band on my wrist and gave me a chocolate, smiling like I was her equal. I remember an old man who gave me his shawl during winter and told me, *"Stay warm, son."*

These weren't grand gestures. But for someone who had nothing, they were everything.

The Cruel Ones

Not everyone on the streets was kind. Some people threw coins at us like we were animals. Some made fun of the way we spoke or smelled. A few even hit or kicked us for being too close to their vehicles. I've seen people take videos of crying children just to get views on their phones, not to offer help.

Sometimes, the cruelty came not from strangers, but from the ones who controlled us—from people like Laxmi Aunty, who fed us but also exploited us.

The Street Kids

I met kids like me from all corners of the city. Some sold flowers. Some shined shoes. Some simply roamed, their eyes lost, their futures blurry. We shared stories, fought over begging spots, played with sticks and stones and imagined lives far better than ours.
Some of them were dreamers. Others were already broken. But all of us had one thing in common—we never chose this life. It chose us.

The NGO Workers and Volunteers

Occasionally, a group of smiling people with ID cards and pamphlets would visit. They'd talk to us about hygiene, education or rights. They gave us soaps, clothes or sometimes food. A few tried convincing Laxmi Aunty to send us to school. She always refused.
Some kids managed to escape through these NGO workers. I don't know where they went, but I hope they found better lives. As for me, I was still waiting for my turn.

The Unseen and the Forgotten

There were others too—the mentally ill who wandered the streets muttering to themselves, the old people abandoned by families, the ragpickers digging through garbage, the construction workers sleeping under flyovers. We were all part of the same unseen city. A city beneath the city.

A world no one writes about. A world everyone walks past.

The streets taught me more than any classroom ever could. They introduced me to every shade of humanity—from its cruellest to its kindest. And every person I met—whether they gave me a coin, a curse, or a conversation—left a mark on my heart.

Because on the streets, people are not just faces. They are stories. And mine is one of them.

Chapter 9 : The Dreams I Dare to Dream

When you live on the streets, dreaming feels like a crime. You're taught to survive, not to hope. To obey, not to imagine. To count coins, not stars.

But no matter how much dust settled on my skin, no matter how many nights I slept hungry, one tiny corner of my heart always dared to dream.

Dreams don't cost anything—and that's the only reason I could afford them.

I Dreamt of a Name, Not a Number

On the streets, no one asks for your name. You're just "Aye chotu!", "Oye bhikhari!" or sometimes, just a nuisance. But I had a name. Deepak. It means "lamp"—a source of light.

I dreamt of a world where people called me by my name, not my condition. Where I didn't have to shout to be heard. Where I mattered—not because of the money I brought home—but simply because I was alive.

I Dreamt of a School Bag

I saw them every day—kids in uniforms, carrying bags bigger than their backs, laughing and running to school. I used to follow them for a while, watching from a distance. I couldn't understand what they were learning, but I wanted to sit in one of those benches, just once.

I dreamt of writing my name on a notebook instead of wiping my nose with old newspapers. Of learning how to read, write and one day, sign my own name on something other than an arrest record or hospital slip.

I Dreamt of a Family Who Waited for Me

Not the kind who counted my coins or punished me when I fell short. I dreamt of a mother who would wait with warm food and a hug. Of a father who would ask me how my day was and not how much I earned.

I dreamt of siblings who would fight over toys, not begging spots. Of a home where love wasn't conditional and where punishments didn't come with hot chilli smoke or locked rooms.

I Dreamt of Festivals, Not Because of Business

Every festival for us meant a change in costumes or products to sell. But I dreamt of celebrating Holi just to throw colours, not to sell them. Of Diwali where I could light a diya without worrying about burning fingers while cooking on a footpath.

I dreamt of a Christmas where I could be the kid receiving chocolates from Santa, not begging outside churches dressed in a second-hand Santa cap.

I Dreamt of a Room With a Door

Not a pavement, not a slum, but a small room of my own. It didn't have to be fancy. Just four walls, a fan and a door that I could shut when the world got too loud.

A place where I could keep my chicken bone from my first earning, my torn teddy and my secrets—safe and untouched.

I Dreamt of a Day Without Fear

Fear was my shadow. Fear of police vans. Fear of Laxmi Aunty. Fear of illness. Fear of losing the little we had. Fear of tomorrow.

I dreamt of a morning where I woke up without worry and a night where I slept without shivering. A day where I didn't have to lie, steal or beg.

I Dreamt of Becoming Someone

Not a beggar. Not a thief. But *someone.*

A driver. A shopkeeper. A teacher. A cook. A person with an ID card, an address and maybe even a bank account. Someone who would walk into a mall without being thrown out. Someone who could help others like me.

Someone who didn't just survive the streets—but escaped them.

I Dreamt... Even When I Knew It Was Dangerous

Because dreams are dangerous when you're poor. They give you hope and hope can make you rebel. It can make you question your life. And questions invite punishment.

But I still dared to dream—quietly, stubbornly. Even when I was laughed at. Even when I was slapped. Even when life crushed every reason to believe.

Because those dreams?

They kept me alive.

They reminded me that I was still human.

And maybe, just maybe, one day… they'll come true.

Chapter 10 : A Day in My Life

Every day in my life looked the same… and yet, no two days were ever truly alike.

The only thing predictable was unpredictability. On the streets, routine isn't something you choose—it's something you survive. So here it is, a day in my life, not from the eyes of a calendar, but from the soul of a boy who woke up to the world before the world woke up to him.

5:30 AM – The Wake-Up Call

No alarm clock, no sunrise. Just the first bark of a street dog, followed by the heavy footsteps of the early sweepers and the sudden honk of the milk van. That was my wake-up call.

Sometimes it was the chill, sometimes the heat, sometimes just the stiffness in my bones from sleeping on broken tiles. I would open my eyes, look up at the sky—gray, blurry and indifferent—and remind myself that I had made it through another night.

Bhumi and Agni would still be curled up beside me under a shared plastic sheet. I'd quietly slip out, careful not to wake them.

6:00 AM – The Mission Starts Early

By now, Laxmi Aunty would be up. She never really slept. Like a hawk, she watched over all of us. She'd give us the first "briefing" of the day—who goes where, who takes which child and which festival or event to target.

Sometimes we'd start with temple gates, sometimes near train stations. She'd comb my hair with her fingers, smear some dirt on my face to make me look pitiful, then give me a crumpled bottle of water and a broken biscuit.
That was breakfast.

8:00 AM – The Signal Life Begins

We'd reach our signal spots as the city started stretching itself awake. Cars would begin piling up. We learned to time the red light perfectly. The moment the light turned red, I'd rush to the windows—head tilted, hands folded, eyes trained to look empty and hungry.

Some would look away. Some would pretend to check their phones. But a few would see me—really see me—and drop coins, food or even a note. On lucky days, I'd get a pack of Frooti or a chocolate. Those were gold.

12:00 PM – Midday Misery

By noon, the sun would start attacking us. Our feet would burn on the hot tar, lips cracked, stomachs rumbling. The signal's kindness would dry up along with the sweat on our backs.

This was also when police vans might show up. We were trained to scatter the moment we saw khaki uniforms. We knew where to hide, how to lie and when to run.

If we got caught, the slaps came free. If not, we'd hide behind hoardings or under flyovers, resting our legs, sipping stolen water and comparing our earnings.

2:00 PM – Food, If Any

Lunch? That depended. If the earnings were decent, Laxmi Aunty might give us a vada pav or a piece of dry roti with salt. Otherwise, we'd search garbage bins outside hotels. Sometimes kind strangers fed us, sometimes we stole leftovers from temple dustbins.

On good days, we'd eat together and laugh at stupid things. On bad days, we'd just chew silence.

4:00 PM – Round Two

Evening was the second shift. We'd change spots, sometimes go to parks or malls. People coming out of work were more generous, especially if we carried a baby in our arms.

This was when I had to act the most. Fake a limp. Cry on command. Make my eyes water. People believed pain when it looked fresh.

7:00 PM – The Count

We'd return home—if you could call it that. A tarpaulin tent in a corner of the slum, near a stinking drain. Laxmi Aunty would call out our names, one by one. We'd hand over every rupee we earned.

No lies. She'd know.

If I earned well, she'd smile and let me sit inside early. If I didn't, I might get a slap or be made to stand outside while others ate.

Dinner was leftover rice, if lucky. Some days just water. But even that was something to be thankful for.

9:00 PM – Stories, Stars and Silence

After dinner, we'd gather. Bhumi would talk about her day, Agni would mimic a rich aunty and Ayush would dream out loud. I'd just listen.

We'd look up at the sky. Count stars. Talk about what clouds look like. Or sometimes, just sit in silence. That silence was oddly comforting—it was the only time of the day when no one demanded anything from us.

11:00 PM – The World Sleeps. So Do We.

We'd lie down—sometimes five of us on one sheet. I'd hug the chicken bone tied around my neck. My first earning. My proof that I existed.

My eyes would close, but not before I whispered my daily wish: "Maybe tomorrow will be different."

That was my day.

Every day.

Over and over.

But within it, hidden like coins in dust, were moments of laughter, slices of hope and dreams stitched into the sky.

Because even in the ugliest parts of life, a little boy still finds something beautiful to hold on to.

Chapter 11 : The First Time I Felt Free

Freedom.

A word I had only heard in slogans on Independence Day, screamed from loudspeakers and pasted on walls. People spoke about it like it was theirs by birthright.

But for me?

It was a distant dream—like owning shoes that actually fit or having a name that wasn't shouted in anger.

And yet, I remember the first time I *felt* free.

It wasn't grand. No music played in the background. But for those few minutes... the world didn't own me.

It was a regular day. Too regular.

Too loud, too dusty, too hopeless.

Laxmi Aunty had been in a foul mood since morning. Bhumi had fallen sick, Ayush had earned nothing the previous day and someone had stolen a plastic sheet from our "home."

Tension was hanging like a sword. We all knew someone was going to get punished—today, it was me.

She slapped me for no reason.

Hard.

Twice.

Then threw the crumpled red cap in my hand and shouted, **"Go to the park. Make yourself useful!"**

I didn't cry. I had learned not to.

But something inside me cracked that day. Not the kind that hurts, but the kind that makes space—like the shell of a bird right before it's born.

I walked away.

But this time, I didn't go to the park.

I just walked.

And walked.

No begging.

No baby in my arms.

No lies on my face.

Just me, barefoot on a sun-baked footpath, the city moving around me like I didn't exist.

I kept walking until the traffic noise faded behind trees and I found myself near the sea.

Yes—the sea.

I had only *heard* about it from other kids. They said it was huge and endless and salty.

They were right.

I stood there, watching waves crash against rocks like they were fighting the whole world.

And for the first time in my life, I didn't feel like a beggar.

I didn't feel like property.

I didn't feel like a puppet with dirt-streaked strings.

I just felt…

Alive.

I took off my dirty shirt.

Ran to the edge.

Felt the water rush past my legs like it had waited forever just to touch me.

I laughed.

Laughed so loud that I scared the birds nearby.

Laughed like a boy who'd found heaven on Earth.

No one told me where to stand.

No one pulled my hand.

No one was watching me with disgust or pity or greed.

In that moment, I belonged only to myself.

I must've stayed there for hours.

I built sand towers and let the waves break them.

I spoke to a dog who seemed lonelier than me.

I lay back and watched the sky change from blue to orange to ink.

It was the first time I realized that silence could be loud and loneliness could feel like peace.

But freedom has a curfew when you don’t have a home.

Eventually, the darkness reminded me of reality.

And fear—my old friend—crept back in.

What if Aunty had found out?

What if Bhumi was crying?

What if I didn’t go back?

I thought about running away. Just disappearing.

But I knew I couldn't—not yet.

So I walked back.

Not as a prisoner, but as someone who had tasted something rare.

Like a caged bird who’d once flown and now knew what the sky *felt* like.
That night, Aunty hit me again.

Harder.

But I didn’t cry.

Because she couldn’t take away what I had felt that day.

She couldn’t drown the sea that had touched my feet.

She couldn’t slap the sky out of my memory.

I had felt something that no slap, no hunger, no pain could erase.

I had felt free.

Not forever.

But enough to keep me going.

And sometimes, enough is everything.

Chapter 12 : Meeting the Stranger Who Changed Everything

I had begged from thousands of people.

Some turned their faces.

Some gave coins.

Some cursed under their breath.

And some… some looked right through me like I was part of the dust.

But then came **her**.

The stranger.

And nothing was ever the same again.

It was just another broken morning.

My stomach growled louder than the city horns.

My feet were cracked, my throat dry. The December wind bit into my skin like it was angry at me for surviving.

I was stationed at a signal near the mall.

It was Bhumi's turn with the baby. Mine was the water bottle and the limp—our daily performance.

The signal turned red. I limped forward with my arm out, eyes low. And then a car window rolled down.

Not unusual.

But what came next was.

She didn't toss coins.

She didn't ask questions.

She just looked at me—really *looked*—with eyes that didn't carry pity, but curiosity. Concern.

I looked up.

She was young. Maybe in her mid-twenties. Hair tied up in a messy bun, glasses slipping down her nose and a soft cotton kurti that smelled faintly like rose water. She wasn't rich-rich, but she had comfort in her bones—something I had never known.

"Hey," she said, softly.

"What's your name?"

No one had asked me that in *years*.

"Deepak," I whispered, barely audible.

Her eyes widened—like it meant something.

"Deepak," she repeated. "That means *light*, right?"

I nodded slowly. My legs trembled. Not from weakness, but because… someone remembered what my name meant.

She didn't give me money.

Instead, she pulled out a small packet from her bag—biscuits, a banana and a sealed juice box.

"Here. You need this more than coins."

I was frozen. Not because of the cold, but because this wasn't charity. It felt… human. Like she wasn't just helping a beggar—she was talking to a *boy*.

I took the packet and said "thank you," unsure whether to stay or leave. But then the light turned green and the cars behind her honked like demons.

She gave me a soft smile and said,

"Stay safe, Deepak."

And then she drove off.

I stood there, holding that packet like it was gold.

Not because of the food.

Because for the first time in forever… someone saw *me*.

Not my dirt. Not my lies. Not my begging act.

Just me.

The next day, I went to the same signal. And the next.

And the next.

She didn't come.

Weeks passed.

I told Bhumi and Ayush about her. They said not to get attached. "Strangers come and go, Deepak. Hope is dangerous for people like us."

But I didn't care.

Because in those three minutes, she gave me something no one else ever had.

She reminded me I was more than my hunger.

More than my clothes.

More than a street-side shadow.

One evening, just as the sun dipped behind the city skyline, I saw that same car.

Same colour. Same plate.

My heart skipped.

It slowed down near the signal.

And I held my breath.

But it wasn't her.

A different driver.

Empty passenger seat.

Still… I smiled.

Because whether I saw her again or not didn't matter anymore.

She had already changed something in me.

She made me want to be worthy of the name I carried—**Deepak**. Light.

Maybe, someday, I'll find her.

Tell her what she did.

Tell her that one small act of kindness, one moment of humanity, gave a beggar boy the courage to start dreaming.

Until then, I carry her voice in my heart.

"Stay safe, Deepak."

And I'm trying.

I really am.

Chapter 13 : The Night I Asked God Why

There's something about night that feels heavier than the day.

During the day, there's noise to distract you—horns, footsteps, yelling vendors, crying babies, clinking coins. But at night… the silence shouts.

And on that night, under the open sky with a torn blanket over my chest and a hundred mosquito bites I couldn't scratch, I couldn't take it anymore.

I looked up, tears welling in my cracked eyes and I asked the only question I had left in me:

"Why, God? Why me?"

I didn't whisper it.

I *screamed* it in my head.

Why was I the one begging at signals?

Why did I sleep on cold footpaths while others tucked themselves into warm beds?

Why was my childhood traded for coins, my laughter stolen for survival?

Why was I born only to *suffer*?

I'd seen temples.

I'd seen people bowing their heads, touching their foreheads to the floor, eyes closed in faith.

I had begged outside those same temples…

…and I had seen people offer laddoos and garlands to idols that couldn't eat,

but ignore the children at their feet who hadn't eaten in *days*.

That night, I couldn't pretend anymore.

If there was a God, I wanted answers.

Not scriptures.

Not rituals.

Just answers.

Bhumi was asleep beside me, her arm wrapped around her stomach. She hadn't eaten dinner. Said she wasn't hungry.

She *lied*. I knew it.

We all did it—gave up food for the younger ones when there wasn't enough.

Ayush was across the road, curled under a rickshaw, mumbling in his sleep. Probably dreaming of running water and biryani.

And I… I just lay there, watching the stars blink back at me like silent witnesses to my pain.

"Are you even real?" I asked the sky.

"If you are, why didn't you stop them?"

The beatings.

The hunger.

The days I sat alone, invisible, with not even a coin to show for it.

I didn't want miracles.

I just wanted to know why my life felt like punishment when I had done *nothing wrong*.

That night, I cried.

Not the loud kind.

The kind where your soul leaks through your eyes and your chest hurts in ways no one can see.

And as I cried, the wind picked up—cold and soft—like a hand brushing my cheek.

Was it God?

Was it just the wind?

I didn't know.

But it made me feel a little less alone.

I wish I could tell you that something magical happened after that night.

That a light appeared.

That my questions were answered.

They weren't.

But something inside me shifted.

Maybe God doesn't answer in words.

Maybe the answers come in the form of people… like that stranger at the signal.

Or in moments… like the warmth of Bhumi's arm when she pulls me closer in her sleep.

Maybe God hides in the little things.

And maybe—just maybe—He cries with us too.

That night didn't fix me.

But it made me *feel* again.

And sometimes, feeling is the first step to healing.

Chapter 14 : The Different Moods of People While Giving Money

People say beggars can't be choosers.

But the truth is, we *feel* everything.

We see the tilt of your head, the curve of your lips, the flicker in your eyes.

And from just that glance — we know what kind of giver you are.

Because money… is never just money.

It comes wrapped in energy.

The Givers Who Smile

These are the rarest.

They don't just give — they *see* you.

Their eyes soften. Their hands reach out.

Sometimes they say "Take care" or pat your head like you're *human* — not an inconvenience.

When they hand over the coin or the note, it feels like warmth. Like a sunray in winter.

I still remember one aunty.

She gave me ten rupees and said, *"I hope you get to eat something nice today."*

I didn't even care about the money.

Her words filled my stomach more than the food did that day.

The Rushed Givers

They give without looking.

Eyes forward. Lips tight. As if the coin is on fire and they just want to be done with it.

I'm not ungrateful — money is money.

But these are the givers who treat you like a traffic bump. You exist, but just barely.

Sometimes, I want to ask them,

"Do you know I have a name? That I laugh too? That I cry at night?"

But I don't.

I take the coin and I whisper thank you to the wind instead.

The Guilty Givers

They look at you like they've seen a ghost.

Eyes darting between your torn clothes and their own expensive watch.

They hesitate.

Then quickly dig into their pocket, drop a coin into your hand and walk away — faster than before.

It's not pity.

It's guilt.

Like your presence reminded them that life is unfair and they don't want to sit with that truth for too long.

Their money comes with weight.

You feel it in your hand, long after they're gone.

The Angry Givers

Oh, these are the hardest.

They give money like they're doing you a favour they'll regret.

Their nose scrunches. Their mouth is tight.

Sometimes they mutter things like *"Go get a job"* or *"Don't use this for drugs."*

They hand the coin with disgust — like they're throwing trash into a bin.

I take it.

But inside, it hurts.

Because I didn't choose this life.

Because I'd give anything to have a job… to earn with dignity… to not have to stretch my hand.

The Fake Givers

Then there are those who pretend.

They smile. They wave. They say *"Sorry, no change"* while sitting in an air-conditioned car worth more than my entire existence.

Some even say, *"God bless you"* without giving a thing.

I nod. I smile. I move on.

But I remember.

The Silent Givers

These people say nothing.

No smile. No frown. Just a quiet transaction.

They look at you like you're the wind — felt, but unseen.

I don't know what they're thinking.

Maybe they're kind. Maybe they're cold.

But sometimes, silence feels like dignity too.

At least they didn't stare. Or laugh. Or take a photo like some others do.

And Then... The Ones Who Don't Give

Not money. Not a glance. Not even the decency to acknowledge your existence.

They roll up the window. Look away. Start scrolling through their phone.

And that, I think, is the hardest to digest.

Not the rejection — but the invisibility.

Over time, I've learned to tell the difference between a ten-rupee note given in love and a hundred-rupee note given in shame.

Some money fills your belly.

Some money breaks your spirit.

But on the street, we take it all — because survival doesn't come with preferences.

Still, I keep the memories of the smiling givers closest to my heart.

Because they reminded me, even for a second, that I'm more than just a beggar.

I'm a boy.

With a name.

And a soul.

Chapter 15 : Years Passed and I Grew from a Boy into a Man

Time never asks if you're ready to grow up.

It doesn't wait for you to dream or to heal.

It just keeps moving. One day melts into another. One signal becomes another. One scar fades and another takes its place.

And somewhere between selling flags and collecting coins, between eating temple prasad and sleeping beside dogs, between Bhumi tying rakhi and Ayush falling sick — I stopped being a boy.

And became a man.

There was no celebration for it.

No cake. No candles.

Just a day when I suddenly realized my shoulders felt heavier — not because of weight, but because of responsibility.

One day, I wasn't the youngest anymore.

I was the one holding someone's hand at the signal.

I was the one teaching a smaller kid how to cry at the right moment, how to stare at people's eyes just enough to make them feel something.

I was the one standing in front when the cops came to shoo us away.

I was the one who stopped asking "Why me?"

And started accepting, "This is me."

My voice got deeper. My arms got stronger.

But my dreams… they remained fragile.

Somewhere in my heart, I still craved to go to school.

To wear clean clothes.

To sit on a chair and be asked, *"What do you want to become when you grow up?"*

But no one asked.

Because on the streets, you're already grown up the day you stop crying.

I remember once, a boy half my age came and sat next to me. He had just started begging.

His nose was runny and his eyes full of fear.

He asked me, "Bhaiya, why do people ignore us?"

I didn't know how to answer.

So I gave him my biscuit and said,

"They don't see us, but I see you. We'll be okay."

That's when I knew.

I had grown.

I still had no ID. No birthday. No certificate to prove I existed. But I existed — in the eyes of those who needed me.

Aunty had grown older. Bhumi had stopped begging and started working at a tea stall.

Ayush was often unwell. And I…

I had become the man of the house that never really was a house.

Some days, I stared at the stars and wondered, *"Is this it? Is this all life has for me?"*

But then I'd see the sunrise — the only free miracle I got to witness every day.

And I'd say to myself,

"Not yet. I'm still alive. I'm still here."

Because even if the world didn't see me grow, I knew — The boy who once cried for milk outside a temple, had grown into a man who gave half his vada pav to a stranger.

And maybe…

Just maybe…

That is what growing up really means.

Chapter 16 : Met a Girl with a Red Ribbon

It was a day like any other.

Sunburned sky, dusty pavement and a hundred indifferent footsteps brushing past me. I had learned by then not to expect anything from a day. When you expect nothing, even a smile feels like a festival.

And that day… a smile did come.

Wearing a red ribbon.

She couldn't have been more than fifteen. Maybe sixteen.

Hair neatly tied, eyes curious but calm — the kind of calm that didn't come from knowing the world, but from believing it could still be beautiful.

She stood across the road, holding a notebook to her chest.

Not a phone. Not a wallet. A notebook.

She looked at me.

Not through me — not around me. **At me.**

It felt strange… to be seen.

I looked down, embarrassed, unsure if I had dirt on my face, or if my torn shirt had caught her attention.

But when I looked up again, she smiled.

Then, she crossed the road.

"Hi," she said, as if we were classmates in some school I never went to.

I didn't reply.

"Your name?" she asked gently.

I hesitated. Nobody *asked*. They just guessed, or shouted, or labelled me "chor," "nalla," "bhikhari."

"…Deepak," I finally whispered.

"Deepak," she repeated, like it was the name of someone important. Then she smiled again. "I'm Rani."

Of course she was.

She looked like one.

And there it was… tied into her braid — a bright, red ribbon.

She didn't give me money.

She gave me something stranger — her time.

She sat next to me, under the shade of a rusted streetlight and opened her notebook. It was filled with poetry. Hindi. English. Words dancing like dreams across ruled pages.

"Do you want to hear one?" she asked.

I nodded.

And as her voice floated between traffic horns and street sellers, I forgot I was sitting on concrete.

Rani came again the next day. And the next.

Sometimes she brought a samosa. Sometimes a book.

Once she gave me a red ribbon of my own — "So you remember me," she said.

I didn't know what love was.

Not the kind in movies.

But I knew what it felt like when someone *chose* to be near you, even when they had every reason not to.

One day, she didn't come.

Then another.

Then a week.

And that's how the streets teach you about life.

People arrive like magic and disappear like smoke.

No goodbye. No explanation.

I kept the ribbon. I tied it to my wrist and some days to my neck.

On days when life felt too heavy, I touched it to remind myself — **I was seen. I was heard. I mattered.**

Even if just for a few afternoons…

to a girl with a notebook and a red ribbon.

Chapter 17 : The Day I Looked for Her

Days had passed — maybe weeks.

The ribbon she gave me was starting to fade, just like her absence.

But something inside me hadn't faded.

Something kept whispering: "Go."

Go find her.

So I did.

I had no address. No phone number. Not even a last name. All I had was a girl's name — *Rani* — and a memory that refused to leave.

I began at the signal where she first appeared, scanning every crowd for a familiar braid, a flash of red, a face that once made my dusty days feel like spring.

She wasn't there.

I waited till sunset.

Then again the next day.

People passed. Thousands of faces.

Most never looked. Some stared too long.

None of them were her.

I walked to the nearest school.

Not one I had ever entered. Not one that would let *me* in. I stood near the gates, watching girls in uniforms file out — some laughing, some tired, none familiar.

A teacher noticed me and frowned. “Why are you loitering here?”

I mumbled, “Looking for someone.”

“Who?”

I didn’t answer.

Because how do you explain to someone that you’re looking for a feeling… a warmth… a piece of your heart?

She shooed me away. I left quietly.

Then I remembered the poems. The notebook.

She used to sit near the bookstore around the corner — the one where second-hand books were sold like old clothes.

Maybe she had come there again?

I ran, barefoot, ignoring the stones and heat of the pavement.

The shopkeeper was sipping chai.

I asked him, “Do you remember a girl? Long braid. Red ribbon. She used to write poems…”

He blinked.

“So many come and go. Don’t remember,” he said.

But then, after a pause, he added, "Wait... Red ribbon? Yes. She came here a few times. Bought an old poetry book... Haven't seen her in a while."

That was all.

A poetry book.

A maybe.

And yet it felt like oxygen.

That night, I sat in my usual spot, under the broken streetlight, staring up at the stars.

Not begging. Not hungry. Just… searching.

I held the red ribbon in my palm and whispered her name.

I realized something then.

Maybe I wasn't looking for her anymore.

Maybe I was looking for the *version of me* she made me believe in.

A version that could be more than a beggar.

More than just a shadow on the street.

She made me want to *be someone.*

And maybe, just maybe… that was the gift she came to give.

Chapter 18 : The First Time I Wanted to Learn Something

The red ribbon no longer felt like just a piece of cloth.

It was a reminder.

Of a girl, yes — but also of a question she left behind:

“Why not you?”

That night, under the flickering streetlamp, I made a promise to the stars:

“I want to learn something. Anything. Just once — I want to feel what it’s like… to know.”

Not just survival. Not just tricks of begging.

But real learning — the kind people in uniforms and bags full of books got to experience.

The next morning, I followed a group of children walking to school.

They laughed freely, backpacks bouncing behind them, uniforms crisp, eyes bright with sleep and dreams.

I didn’t walk with them — just behind, like a silent shadow.

I watched how they entered the school gate.

How they greeted the guard.

How the bell rang and they disappeared inside.

I stood outside for hours. Watching.

Dreaming.

That afternoon, I gathered every coin I had saved and walked to a small stationery shop.

“I want a notebook,” I said, nervous.

The shopkeeper glanced at me — barefoot, dusty, unsure.

“Why?”

“To write,” I said.

“Letters.”

He gave a half-smile, handed me a cheap notebook and a pencil.

No questions asked.

That night, under my usual streetlight, I opened the notebook.

Blank pages stared back at me.

I didn’t know how to write properly. But I remembered the letters from signboards, hoardings and book covers.

So I started slowly.

I copied the English alphabet from a discarded wrapper.

I traced the Hindi letters from a newspaper I found in the trash.

A B C D...

अ आ इ ई...

I had no teacher. But I had patience.

I had hunger — not just for food, but for meaning.

Each letter felt like a little victory.

Bhumi saw me writing and laughed.

“Since when did you become a schoolboy?” she teased.

“I don’t know,” I said honestly, “but it feels nice.”

She sat next to me, curious. Agni joined too. Soon we all were trying to draw letters.

I became their teacher — without even knowing everything myself.

We copied street signs. We asked fruit vendors what the names of fruits were.

We learned by listening. Watching. Repeating.

Slowly, the streets turned into our classroom.

The city became our school.

And for the first time in my life… I wasn't just a beggar.

I was a *student*.

Chapter 19 : A Word Becomes a World

A week had passed since I scribbled my first alphabet.

My notebook was now filled with uneven lines, half-drawn letters, misspelled words and tiny doodles.

But to me, it felt like a masterpiece.

Each stroke of pencil felt like a new muscle forming — inside my mind.

I didn't just want to learn anymore.

I wanted to *understand.*

One day, as I sat under my usual light post, trying to sound out the word **"Ba-na-na"** from a fruit vendor's crate, a man in a white kurta stopped near me.

"You're trying to read that?" he asked, curious.

I nodded.

He sat beside me without hesitation.

"Show me what else you've written."

I hesitated, but handed him my notebook.

He flipped through the pages. His face didn't mock me. He didn't laugh like others.

He simply smiled — soft, slow, approving.

"You know," he said, "I teach kids in the evenings, just two streets from here. Come if you want to learn properly."

I looked at him in disbelief.

"Will you… really teach me?"

"Yes," he said. "No uniform needed. Just bring your notebook. And that same hunger in your eyes."

That evening, I didn't beg.

I didn't wait at the signal.

I waited outside the community hall, heart racing, fingers clutched around my pencil like it was gold.

When the door opened, I saw a room full of kids — some barefoot like me, some in worn clothes, but all with notebooks and eyes glowing.

The man — we called him **Masterji** — welcomed me in.

"Everyone starts somewhere," he said. "Let this be your start."

That night I learned what a *sentence* was.

How letters made words and words made meaning.

I read my first sentence out loud:

"My name is Deepak."

I couldn't stop smiling.

For the first time, my identity wasn't just written on the face of my misery.

It was written — in letters, in my own voice.

Learning became my secret power.

I begged during the day — but I *learned* in the evening.

I still lived on the streets — but my mind began living in a different place.

I taught Bhumi and Agni whatever I learned.

We'd make up little quizzes, write each other's names, guess letters on signboards.

Even Laxmi Aunty noticed the change.

"What are you doing with that notebook all day?" she snapped one evening.

"Trying to become someone," I muttered.

She didn't reply. Just stared. Maybe confused. Maybe proud.

That was the beginning of something I never imagined I could reach— The beginning of **hope**.

Chapter 20 : When Words Opened Doors

Weeks rolled by.

Every day after begging, I'd rush to the small room where Masterji taught.

That dim-lit room had no fan, just cracked walls and chalk dust. But it felt like heaven.

I started reading signboards out loud. Spelling ingredients on the packets people threw away.

Sometimes, I'd sit by the tea stall and copy words from newspapers, though the headlines often made no sense.

I didn't care.

I was chasing meaning.

One afternoon, I was standing outside a café, trying to pronounce a board that read:

"Wanted: Helper – Must know basic English."

I didn't realize someone had been watching me.

"Hey, kid," said a voice from behind.

I turned around. A man with rolled-up sleeves and tired eyes stood there — probably the café manager.

"You trying to read that?"

I nodded, embarrassed.

"Where did you learn to read?"

"I go to Masterji's class," I said quickly, "I can write my name too!"

"Hmm." He looked at me like he was deciding something heavy.

"You want a job? It's nothing big. Just cleaning tables, bringing water. I'll give you food and... ₹100 a day. And if you keep learning, I'll teach you more."

My heart stopped.

Not because of the money.

But because **someone believed in me**.

That evening, I walked into the café not as a beggar...

But as **Deepak – the boy with a name, a notebook and now, a job.**

The uniform was an old apron that reached my ankles.

My hands shook the first time I carried a tray.

But no one laughed.

They smiled.

And every time someone said, "Thank you," I'd whisper back,

"You're welcome,"

...even if I pronounced it wrong.

That night, I didn't beg.

I didn't even need to.

I went home with money **I earned,**

Bread **I didn't beg for,**

And dignity **I had never felt before**.

Bhumi hugged me so tight I thought she'd crack my ribs.

Ayush slapped my back like a proud older brother.

Even Laxmi Aunty didn't say much — just served me extra dal without a word.

I slept like I never had before.

Not with a full stomach.

But with a full heart.

Chapter 21 : Balancing the Two Worlds

Mornings began with me wiping tables and cleaning cups at the café.

Evenings were for chalk, slates and Masterji's patient voice.

By day, I was a worker. By dusk, a student.

Some of the café customers started noticing me.

"Your English is getting better," one lady told me with a smile.

One day, a man handed me an old storybook.

"I read this when I was your age. Try it," he said.

I treasured that book like gold.

At night, Bhumi and Agni would gather around me.

I'd read aloud whatever I had learned — even if I stumbled.

They clapped anyway.

Sometimes, I taught them letters.

We turned it into a game.

Our slum became a classroom, with laughter as our school bell.

But the balance wasn't always easy.

Some days, I spilled tea at work or nodded off in class.

Some nights, hunger returned and Laxmi Aunty would yell.

One day, a customer insulted me — called me "a street boy."

That stung more than anything.

I went home and curled up with the storybook, pressing it against my chest.

"I don't belong anywhere," I whispered into the darkness.

The next morning, I went to Masterji and asked,

"Will I always be like this? Half of everything, whole of nothing?"

He didn't answer right away. He took a deep breath and said,

"Deepak, you're learning to swim in two oceans at once. It's hard, yes. But someday, you'll be the bridge between them."

That day, I didn't spill tea.

That night, I read an entire page without stuttering.

I was still poor.

Still struggling.

But for the first time, **I felt like I belonged to something bigger than my pain.**

Chapter 22 : The Voice I Never Knew I Had

The calendar turned, unnoticed.

Seasons changed, unnoticed.

But something inside me — that was changing.

And it could no longer be ignored.

By then, I had become a quiet fixture at the café. The regulars started smiling at me. Some even asked my name.

One of them was Mr. Suresh Nambiar — a well-dressed man with kind eyes and a habit of reading the newspaper front to back, every single day.

I always noticed how he tipped more than necessary.

How he folded his napkin neatly after every meal.

And how, once, he gave his entire lunchbox to a street kid standing by the window.

One afternoon, he called out softly, “Boy, can I ask you something?”

I straightened up.

“Yes, sir.”

“Do you study?”

“Yes, sir. In the evenings.”

“Do you read?”

"Yes, sir. I try."

"Do you speak?"

"Sometimes… to the mirror," I said, a little embarrassed.

He smiled gently.

"Would you speak in front of people?"

That question startled me.

Three days later, I was standing in a school auditorium packed with students.

Mr. Nambiar, as it turned out, was a trustee there — organizing events on social change.

"Talk about your life," he had told me.

"Just tell your truth. That's more powerful than anything rehearsed."

I wore a simple shirt, borrowed from the café owner's son.

My hands trembled behind the podium.

The mic squeaked. The crowd hushed.

I looked down.

Then I looked up.

And then… I spoke.

"My name is Deepak. I'm 14.

I begged at signals.

I washed milk out of gutters to drink.

But I also know the alphabet.

I know kindness from strangers.

And I've learned that stories… can change people."

The room was so silent, I could hear my own heart pounding.

I spoke for just five minutes.

But it felt like five lifetimes pouring out of my chest.

When I finished, people clapped.

Some stood.

One girl in the front row wiped her tears.

Mr. Nambiar walked up to me and whispered,

"Now, they'll never forget your name."

That evening, I walked back to my slum with no extra money, no medals, no rewards.

But my chest felt light.

And my soul? Loud.

Because for the first time, **the boy who once begged to be seen… was finally heard.**

Chapter 23 : A Chance to Rewrite My Story

After the speech, the claps faded.

The students filed out.

The lights dimmed.

But something lingered in the air — something I had never felt before: **hope**. Hope that others believed in me.

Back at the café, life went on.

Wiping tables. Smiling at customers.

But now, people greeted me differently.

They called me by my name.

They said things like, “You spoke so well!” and “You made me cry, kid.”

Even the café manager, usually stone-faced, placed a hand on my shoulder and said, “You made us proud.”

One week later, Mr. Nambiar returned — not with tea or tips, but with an envelope.

He handed it to me.

“Open it when you’re alone,” he said.

I waited until night.

I walked to my quiet corner near the temple wall, sat under the streetlight and slowly opened the envelope with shaky fingers.

Inside was a letter.

"To Deepak —

This is a full scholarship to St. Arun's Foundation School for the Underprivileged.

It includes tuition, books, uniform and a meal every day.

We've seen your courage.

Now let us see your future."

Below was a signature. A seal.

And a sentence that made my eyes fill with water:

"You are not invisible anymore."

I didn't cry loudly.

I didn't jump or scream.

I just sat there, the letter clutched to my chest like it was my heartbeat.

Because finally, someone had given me a way out.

Not a coin.

Not a biscuit.

But a key.

To a classroom.

To a desk.

To a future.

That night, I told Bhumi and Agni.

They hugged me tighter than ever.

Even Laxmi Aunty, though she grumbled about "wasting time in books," served me the biggest portion of rice.

I lay awake for hours.

Not in fear.

But in imagination.

I imagined wearing a uniform.

Carrying a school bag.

Writing essays, raising my hand in class, maybe even making friends who didn't start their days with hunger.

I imagined standing on a stage again — not just to tell people I survived...

But to tell them how I succeeded.

That night, for the first time ever, I didn't ask God, "Why me?"

I whispered a different question into the sky:

"What if... this is just the beginning?"

Chapter 24 : The Boy in the Borrowed Shoes

The day had finally arrived.

I stood in front of the mirror hanging on the café's back wall — cracked, old, but still clear enough to show a boy who didn't look like the same Deepak anymore.

My shirt was too big and my trousers were held up with a string.

My shoes were borrowed from Ayush, who insisted they were lucky.

My hair had been oiled and combed flat by Bhumi.

And tucked into my notebook was the letter that changed everything.

I held onto it like it was a passport to another planet.

The school was bigger than any temple I'd ever seen.

White walls. Glass doors. Kids in perfect uniforms laughing with school bags in hand.

A world that smelled like sanitizer and ink — not sweat and survival.

As I stepped inside, every footfall felt heavier.

The marble floors echoed my awkwardness.

Eyes turned. Whispers followed.

"Who's that?"

"Why is his shirt like that?"

"Is he new?"

I kept my head down and handed the letter to the receptionist.

She looked up, a little surprised, then smiled warmly.

"Ah… you're Deepak. Come. We've been expecting you."

My class was 7B.

I walked in.

The teacher introduced me.

"Class, this is Deepak. He's joining us from the foundation program. I hope you'll make him feel welcome."

A few students nodded. One girl smiled. Most went back to their own world.

I took a seat at the last bench — quiet, stiff, trying not to look lost.

The emotional contrast hit me hard.

At signals, I fought to catch attention.

Here, I fought to avoid it.

Back home, noise was constant — laughter, fights, traffic.

Here, silence was required. Controlled. Almost too clean.

In the streets, I could talk to anyone.

Here, I didn't know what to say.

Every time a question was asked in class, my hand wanted to rise — but my past made it tremble.

What if I say something wrong?

What if they laugh?

What if they see I don't belong?

But something shifted during English period.

The teacher read out a story — one about a boy who wanted to fly. Then she asked,

"Can anyone guess what the boy's real dream was?"

No one answered.

I raised my hand — slowly.

Heads turned. The teacher nodded.

I said,

"Ma'am… I think the boy didn't just want to fly.

He wanted to be seen.

And remembered."

The room went silent.

And for the first time,

I wasn't invisible.

I was a student. A voice. A possibility.

Later that day, during recess, the girl who had smiled earlier came up to me.

"That was a nice answer. I'm Meera."

I just nodded — shy but smiling.

By the time the bell rang, I had made two new friends.

They didn't ask where I came from.

They only asked if I'd sit with them tomorrow.

When I walked back home that evening,

My shoes were dusty.

My bag was empty.

But my heart…

My heart was full of something new.

Belonging.

Chapter 25 : Five Years of Becoming Deepak

If you ever asked me what changed me the most — I wouldn't say the scholarship. Or the schoolbag. Or even the classroom.

I'd say: **Time**.

Because five years in school didn't just teach me subjects.

They taught me *myself*.

Year 1: The Year of Silence

I was still learning how to hold a pen the right way.

I wrote like the paper might judge me.

Words came slowly. English felt like chewing stones.

Lunch breaks were awkward. Uniforms felt like they belonged to someone else's world.

I hid my past like it was a crime.

But I never missed a single day.

I showed up — in rain, heat, fever or with bruises no one asked about.

Every night, I studied under dim street lights or borrowed café bulbs.

And every morning, I woke up hungry — not just for food, but for something I didn't know how to name.

Maybe it was **dignity**.

Year 2: The Year of Curiosity

I started asking questions.

So many that teachers joked, "Deepak doesn't just want answers — he wants reasons."

I joined the school library and disappeared into pages of worlds I never knew existed — Africa, space, ancient India, the ocean floor.

At lunch, I shared my tiffin with a boy who once mocked my accent. He became my best friend.

I even joined the poetry club. I never read my poems aloud, though.

I was still learning how to trust my own voice.

Year 3: The Year of Dual Lives

By then, I was living two lives.

Morning to afternoon: Student.

Evening to night: Café cleaner, part-time errand boy, elder brother.

I scrubbed dishes with one hand and solved math problems in my head with the other.

My teachers noticed. Not just the struggle — the spark.

One day, the principal called me aside and said, "Your poverty doesn't define you, Deepak. Your grit does."

I held onto those words like a prayer.

Year 4: The Year of Discovery

This was the year I found my superpower — *public speaking*.

One teacher forced me to audition for a debate competition.

I panicked. Almost ran.

But something inside me whispered: *Speak.*

And when I did — my words weren't polished. But they were pure.

Not memorized. But *lived.*

I spoke about growing up on the streets. About watching life from the margins.

The audience didn't just clap.

They stood.

After that, I was invited to speak at events, seminars, foundations.

The boy who once begged at signals… was now *heard* in auditoriums.

Year 5: The Year of Becoming

High school.

The final year.

The year of board exams, pressure, dreams and farewells.

I studied like a man possessed.

Not to top the class — but to not let my people down.

I wanted to be the first in my family, my basti — maybe even my bloodline — to finish school.

I wanted Bhumi to know her sacrifices meant something.

I wanted Laxmi Aunty to smile without guilt.

I wanted Ayush and Agni to see one of us *make it*.

And I did.

Top 5 in my school.

Scholarship extended.

Admission letter from a reputed college.

When the results came out, I didn't cry.

I laughed.

Loud. Mad. Free.

Then I walked to the same signal where I once begged, sat down, looked up at the sky and whispered:

"We did it."

Chapter 26 : Between Lecture Halls and Late Shifts

College felt like another planet.

No bells every 40 minutes.

No uniforms. No fixed benches.

Just faces. New ones. Polished ones. Privileged ones.

I walked into my first college classroom with a second-hand backpack, three pens, a water bottle — and the weight of two worlds on my shoulders.

The Campus

It was massive — trees older than the country, canteens buzzing with debates on politics, movies, love stories.

I often sat at the back. Quiet. Watching.

Watching people who hadn't tasted hunger the way I had.

Some arrived in cars.

Some left in taxis.

I left in thoughts.

The Part-Time Hustle

To cover the little things the scholarship couldn't — like stationery, a samosa on tough days, a phone recharge — I started working evenings.

Book café, just walking distance from college.

6:00 PM to 10:30 PM. Monday to Saturday.

I wiped tables, arranged books, handled the counter — but what I secretly loved most was the silence between orders. The scent of old pages. The poetry resting on shelves.

The café owner — an old man with tired eyes and a kind heart — once told me:

"You don't belong here, mopping floors."

I smiled and said, "I do… but not forever."

The Balancing Act

College in the morning.

Work in the evening.

Assignments past midnight.

Sleep? A luxury.

There were days I skipped meals.

Days I missed class to pick up an extra shift.

Days I wondered, *"Am I stretching too far?"*

But every time I sat in that classroom — exhausted but determined — I remembered:

I wasn't here to chase a degree.

I was chasing **dignity**.

Finding Friends

In second semester, something softened in me.

I started speaking more. Laughing — really laughing.

I found two people who made college feel like home:

Rhea — a chai-lover and sociology student who questioned the world like I did.

Karan — a hostel boy with bad jokes and the best heart. He always saved me a seat.

They didn't pity me.

They didn't prod.

They treated me like I belonged — and that meant everything.

Once, Rhea asked me about my past.

I told her — not everything, but enough.

She didn't flinch.

She just said, "You're the strongest person I know."

Moments That Mattered

I won a college speech contest — "Breaking the Cycle of Poverty." That title felt personal.

The café let me host open mic nights once a month. I read my poems — nervous voice, full heart.

On my 21st birthday, the café staff and my friends threw me a surprise party.

My first birthday celebration.

And sometimes, when I passed children begging at signals, I slipped notes inside their food packets.

"You are more than what the world tells you. Wait for your sunrise."

The Invisible War

But not everything was perfect.

There were days I sat alone in crowded rooms — listening to stories of foreign vacations, Diwali gifts, childhood cartoons I never watched.

Conversations that reminded me — I was still climbing.

Nights when I stared at the ceiling fan and whispered,

"How far do I have to go before I stop feeling small?"

But even then — I kept going.

The End of College — and a Beginning

Three years flew by in a blur of books, bills and becoming.

I graduated with distinction.

The café offered me a managerial post.

But I was looking for something more. Something that felt like *purpose*.

During campus placement, the college gave me a recommendation letter — for a journalism internship.

And that day, as I stood with the letter in my hand, looking ahead, I didn't just feel proud.

I felt *ready*.

Not just for success.

For **meaning**.

Chapter 27 : First Step into the Real World

The day I got the email, I read it six times.

Subject: Congratulations – You're Selected!

A media startup — small but sharp — focused on human stories, social change, grassroots journalism. They had seen me speak at a youth event, sharing my journey from traffic signals to a graduation stage.

They didn't want just a résumé. They wanted *my voice.*

It wasn't a big salary. But it wasn't about the money.

It was about *belonging.*

It was about finally being invited to the table — not just knocking from the outside.

The Office

The office was inside a shared co-working space — beanbags, black coffee, glass walls filled with scribbles and slogans.

On my first day, I walked in wearing the neatly ironed shirt I'd bought months ago from my café salary and the shoes my friend had gifted me after graduation.

I was quiet. Observant. Just like my first day of college.

Only this time — I walked in with *stories in my eyes.*

A senior editor shook my hand and smiled, "We've been waiting to hear your stories."

Learning the Ropes

The job was intense.

Morning meetings.

Field interviews.

Deadlines.

Writing. Rewriting. Then rewriting again.

I was assigned stories that lived on the margins —

Child labourers.

Slum schools.

Daily-wage workers.

Forgotten freedom fighters.

These weren't just articles.

They were mirrors.

Every wrinkled face reminded me of someone I knew.

Every barefoot child reminded me of my own reflection in muddy puddles outside rich restaurants.

It wasn't just journalism.

It was personal.

The Imposter Feeling

But not all days were brave ones.

My colleagues had shiny degrees. Spoke in flawless English. Tossed around terms like "narrative building" and "socioeconomic disparity."

Sometimes I sat silently — afraid to speak.

Afraid my grammar would give me away.

Afraid my accent wasn't "professional" enough.

But slowly — gently — I understood something:

They had vocabulary.

I had lived truth.

And when I did speak… people listened.

Not because I talked *about* poverty.

But because I spoke *from* it.

The First Published Article

The title was bold:

"I Once Begged on These Streets. Now I Tell Their Stories."

It went viral.

Emails poured in.

Some thanked me.

Some offered help.

Some admitted they had never seen street children as more than background noise.

My old café owner printed it out and framed it.

Hung it on the café wall near the counter.

Laxmi Aunty, always half-sceptical, looked at it and said,

"So… people pay you for *talking* now, ha?"

I laughed.

And then, quietly… I cried too.

Because that moment meant something only I could understand.

A Turning Point

One afternoon, while covering a story in a slum school, a small boy tugged at my sleeve.

He looked up at me and asked,

"Bhaiya, you came here in a car? Are you rich now?"

I knelt down. Smiled.

And said,

"No, I'm not rich. I'm just growing."

Chapter 28 : A Story Too Close

It was an ordinary Tuesday morning when my editor walked in holding a thin manila folder.

"Deepak," she said, "we're starting a series on urban poverty and child exploitation. I want you to lead one of the stories."

I nodded and took the file.

The moment I flipped it open, a strange chill crept down my spine.

Location: Sion East – Near Signal

My old signal.

Where I once stood, holding Bhumi's hand.

Where Ayush taught me to beg.

Where a woman with kind eyes once gave me my first five hundred rupee note — like she was handing me hope.

"You okay?" my editor asked.

I smiled, faintly. "Yes… I know the place. Very well."

Back to the Signal

I went alone.

No camera crew. No mic. Just a notepad, my voice recorder and a heart packed tight with ghosts I hadn't spoken to in years.

I stood across the signal and just watched.

It hadn't changed.

Still dusty. Still chaotic. Still loud.

But now I wasn't barefoot.

I had clean clothes. A press ID. A purpose.

I hadn't come to beg.

I had come to *listen.*

The Girl in the Green Dress

She was the first face I saw clearly — a little girl in a green dress too big for her frame, hair like a messy nest, holding a plastic flower faded by sun and rejection.

She went from car to car, tapping windows.

I saw myself in her, too easily.

I crouched down as she neared me.

"Kya naam hai tumhara?" (what is your name) I asked.

She looked at me, unsure.

Then said, in a voice smaller than her: "Geeta."

I handed her a bottle of water. She stared at it like I'd handed her gold.

"Main journalist hoon," (I am journalist) I said softly. "Tumse kuch baatein karni hai." (I want to talk with you something)

She looked around. Nervous. Then slowly nodded.

Behind the Curtains

For the next week, I traced her story.

Her caretaker was a woman named Savita — she managed five kids like they were currency.

Made them beg. Hit them when they didn't bring enough.

Geeta's life… it echoed mine so closely, it hurt.

I felt rage.

I felt helpless.

But most of all, I felt **responsible**.

I documented everything; The corners they were stationed at, The earnings, The bruises, The routine, The trap and in all of it, the thought that haunted me most was: *This could've still been me.*

If just one hand hadn't pulled me out.

Writing Through Tears

Back at my desk, I tried to type.

But the words came broken.

My hands shook.

Tears fell freely.

This wasn't just an assignment.
This was *my story*, told in someone else's voice.

The title I finally chose was:

"Her Name Is Geeta and I Was Her Once."

The Impact

The article spread like wildfire.

A rescue NGO reached out within days.

By the end of that week, Geeta and the others were pulled from Savita's claws and placed in a safe shelter.

Before she left, I visited her.

She saw me and ran — full speed — into my arms.

"Bhaiya," (brother) she whispered, "main bhi school jaungi na?" (Will I be going to school?)

My throat closed up.

All I could do was nod.

That day, I didn't go back to the office.

I walked to the sea, found an empty bench and just sat.

I looked up.

And whispered,

"Thank you. For giving me a story that became someone else's salvation."

Chapter 29 : The Microphone and the Mission

The email came on a rainy evening — the kind where the world feels like it's pausing to listen.

Subject: Invitation to Speak at the National Youth Summit – Change Makers 2025

I stared at the screen.

Frozen.

They had read my article — *"Her Name is Geeta and I Was Her Once."*

They wanted me to speak.

Not just as a journalist.

As a symbol. Of change. Of resilience. Of what's possible when someone gets a second chance.

And suddenly, I felt like that little boy at the signal again — standing in front of a car, hoping someone would roll the window down.

My heart raced.

I wasn't sure I could do it.

But something deeper than fear whispered:

"Do it. For Geeta. For Bhumi. For Ayush. For Agni. For the boy you once were."

The Day of the Summit

I wore a plain white kurta.

No designer label. No brand.

Just clean. Ironed. Real.

The auditorium was packed — young minds, thinkers, activists, dreamers. People who could change the world or already were.

And there I was, about to walk on stage — not as a beggar, not as a survivor — but as someone *invited* to speak.

I stood behind the microphone.

It took me thirty long seconds to say the first word. Then I began:

"I was born into wealth.

Then abandoned into poverty.

Then I begged.

Then I survived.

Then someone noticed me.

And now…

I stand before you holding a microphone instead of a begging bowl."

The room went silent.

Still.

I told them everything.

The sting of red chilies.

The chicken bone I wore like an amulet.

The girl with the red ribbon.

The taste of temple milk.

The nights under trucks.

And finally — Geeta.

The Room Stood Still

When I finished, they stood.

They clapped.

Some wept.

Some hugged me.

Some just held their hearts.

A woman in her fifties came up with folded hands and said:

"My son complains about hostel food. I'm going to make him read your story tonight."

I smiled.

And felt something shift inside me.

But the surprises weren't over.

A Scholarship and a Mission

Backstage, a man walked up — kind eyes, old-world grace. He was the director of an education foundation.

"We've been following your work," he said. "Your writing is raw. Unfiltered. It *matters.*"

Then came words I never expected to hear:

"We'd like to offer you a full scholarship to pursue a Master's in Social Journalism abroad. And if you choose not to, we'd be honoured to sponsor your grassroots storytelling work here in India."

I couldn't speak. My throat was a knot.

I just nodded. Not yes. Not no. Just gratitude.

I didn't take the scholarship — not because it wasn't a dream, but because… I *had* a dream here.

A mission.

A story still unfolding — mine and those like mine.

That night, I stood on a small hotel balcony, the city blinking below like a constellation.

I looked up at the sky — the same sky that once watched me sleep on footpaths.

And I whispered: **"Maybe… just maybe…**

I was never meant to stay broken."

Chapter 30 : The Girl with the Red Ribbon (Again)

It was a regular Sunday.

I'd been invited to speak at a small NGO that worked with children living on the streets. The place felt achingly familiar — rusted tin roofs, plastic slippers too big for tiny feet, laughter echoing off wounds no one could see.

I was halfway through a story with the kids when someone tapped my shoulder.

"Sir, someone outside wants to meet you. She says… she knows you."

I stepped out, expecting maybe an old teacher… someone from the shelter days.

But there she was.

Leaning against a faded blue scooter, wearing a yellow kurta.

Hair tied in a bun. And a red ribbon — not in her hair this time, but wrapped around her wrist… like a secret she never let go.

Time didn't slow down.

It stopped.

Burning afternoons at the signal.

Running barefoot with coins.

Her last glimpse — chasing a moving car, disappearing into the crowd.

My voice cracked.

“Rani?”

She smiled.

That same crooked, mischievous smile that used to light up my darkest evenings.

“You remember me?” she asked.

I let out a shaky laugh.

“I’ve tried to forget many things in life, Rani. But never you.”

We sat beneath a banyan tree nearby and the hours dissolved like sugar in chai.

She told me everything.

How her relatives took her away to a new city.

How she finished school, studied social work.

How she came back — not for comfort, but to serve. To find faces like ours once were.

“I looked for you,” she said softly. **“Many times.”**

“So did I,” I whispered. **“I asked God about you once. The night I had no answers.”**

She smiled gently.

“Maybe He was just waiting for the right time.”

Becoming Friends Again

We started meeting often after that.

NGO events.

Evenings over cutting chai.

Sometimes we didn't even talk — just sat in silence, letting the past breathe between us.

She still wore red ribbons — not just on her wrist, but around lunchboxes for kids at the shelter. It had become her thing. A symbol. Of survival. Of softness. Of remembering who she was.

With her, laughter came easy. Like time had taken a long walk but left our bond untouched. We weren't those same kids anymore — but we still carried their souls. Just with fewer bruises and more courage.

One day, she looked at me and asked,

"Do you think… broken people can fall in love?"

I met her gaze — steady, unafraid, full of everything I couldn't say out loud.

"Only broken people know how to hold the pieces gently."

And for the first time in years…

I felt whole.

Chapter 31 : When Friendship Begins to Bloom

We started seeing each other more often.

Not because we planned to.

But because… somehow, life kept weaving us into the same moments.

An NGO seminar.

One of my talks.

Her delivering meals to kids with that giant steel dabba in her hand.

And every time, in the middle of a room full of voices and movement, my eyes would find hers — like a compass that had stopped spinning.

Always seeking.

Always anchoring.

The Little Moments

It wasn't the big gestures.

It was the little things that started to shift something inside me — something quiet, something steady.

When she forgot to eat (which was often), I'd magically show up with vada pav and a bottle of mango juice — the same combo we used to share when our feet were still dusty and our dreams didn't have names.

When I burnt out from work, running from deadline to deadline, she'd appear at my door — soaked in rain or sunshine, holding haldi doodh (turmeric milk) and that signature frown of hers.

"You don't have to save the world in one day, Deepak," she'd mutter, fixing my collar like a stubborn sister or… maybe something more.

"I'm not trying to save the world," I'd reply. **"Just trying to save that boy who once begged outside Signal's."**

We started texting into the night. Not with intent, just… with honesty.

Random memories.

The kids we were working with.

Her favourite poems.

My journal scribbles.

One night, she messaged:

"Do you remember the day I tied a red ribbon on your wrist and called you my friend?"

I replied:

"Still have it. Still am."

The Day It Changed

It was raining hard that afternoon — the kind of Mumbai rain that feels like it's falling sideways.

I found her standing outside my office, drenched to the bone, shivering… and smiling.

"The shelter was flooding," she said. **"I went to help. Thought I'd stop by and see you after."**

I rushed her inside, handed her a towel, made chai just how she liked it — extra ginger, barely any sugar.

She cupped the glass between her hands, steam rising between us.

Our eyes met. And for a moment, the world hushed. Not awkward silence —

But the kind that exists only between two people who've tasted the same hunger, the same helplessness… and survived it.

"You don't have to always show up strong, Rani," I whispered.

"Neither do you," she replied, her voice barely above the rain outside.

And in that silence, something bloomed — not loud, not urgent, just real.

Love didn't arrive with violins. It arrived with a damp umbrella.

With a towel shared between friends.

With the way her presence made my breath slow down.

A Walk Home

I walked her home under an old, torn umbrella that barely covered us.

The rain kept falling — but it didn’t feel cold anymore.

Outside her door, she paused. Looked at me like she had something wrapped in her chest for years.

“Do you think we’ve both come too far to start something new?”

I smiled, heart pounding.

“Maybe we haven’t come this far for nothing.”

Chapter 32 : When Love Finds Its Voice

Weeks turned into months.

What began as a gentle reunion with Rani started blooming into something deeper. Quietly. Unhurried. Like two rivers meeting after years of carving their own paths.

It wasn't that we didn't know what this was.

We did.

But some love stories don't arrive with fireworks.

They arrive as whispers.

As shared silences.

As glances that say more than words ever could.

The Almost-Confession

One evening, I invited Rani to this small café near Marine Drive. A hidden gem — run by an old couple who served chai in kulhads and pasted poems on the walls like love notes to strangers.

I had planned to tell her everything that night.

That she had become my calm after the chaos.

That her laughter was the only sound that could silence the storms in my head.

That every time I prayed — really prayed — her name showed up before mine.

I was ready.

But just as I began, she cut in with a laugh that was a little too quick, a little too careful.

"Remember that little boy at the shelter last week? He asked me if I had a husband like you…"

I blinked. "Like me?"

She nodded, eyes darting toward the kulhad she was holding.

"I told him we were just friends. But he didn't buy it. He said, 'No Didi… you look at him the way mummy used to look at papa.'"

She tried to brush it off with a laugh, but her fingers betrayed her — tracing invisible patterns on the table.

I smiled. My heartbeat had already skipped ahead.

"And what did you say to that?" I asked.

She finally looked up. No laughter this time. Just truth.

"I told him… maybe even I didn't believe me."

That was it.

That's how we confessed.

Not with the words "I love you," but with a thousand smaller truths that carried more weight than any declaration ever could.

Our First Date That Felt Like Forever

From that day, something shifted.

And yet… everything stayed beautifully the same.

We still argued about silly things — like who made better pani puri: the guy near Churchgate or the one behind CST.

We still teased each other, still dreamed like kids making castles out of nothing.

Only now, the spaces between us had softened.

The hand-holding didn't need a reason.

And the hugs… they stayed a little longer than they used to.

Sometimes, in the middle of a sentence, we'd just pause — not because we forgot what we were saying, but because we found each other's eyes.

And smiled.

Like we were both saying without words:

"You're my favourite story."

Chapter 33 : A Wedding Beneath the Open Sky

I never wanted a grand wedding. Neither did Rani.

We'd both seen too much of the world to be moved by gold or glitter. We'd watched people worship rituals while forgetting the essence of relationships — families that spent lakhs on lighting but never lit up their child's loneliness. We wanted something quieter. Something true.

So we chose a rooftop garden — not at a resort, but at the very shelter where I once slept curled up against a wall and where Rani had wiped my tears with fingers that trembled but never stopped reaching.

That place had held our worst days. It had also watched us heal. It deserved to see us rise.

Fairy lights danced across bamboo poles. Clay lamps flickered along the edges like blessings whispered by the earth. The air smelled of marigold and wild jasmine — not from a florist's catalogue, but from children who picked them barefoot, laughing, their hands full of colour and mischief.

Our baraatis weren't distant relatives wrapped in heavy silks. They were the kids we'd mentored — shirt buttons missing, anklets jingling, eyes shining. Bhumi, Ayush and Agni were there too — still holding hands like always, somewhere between our past and future.

Bhumi arrived with her husband, who runs a tea stall, and they now live in Pune. Ayush came with his wife, who works as a cook in various households, and they are settled in Nashik. Agni too came along with her husband, who drives an auto-rickshaw in Surat. All three have built a stable life and are happily living with their families.

And then there was the old couple from the café — the same two who once gave me chai on a cold night, no questions asked. They brought us two clay kulhads as a gift, etched with a shaky but perfect "D + R."

Laxmi Aunty sat in the front row in her frayed shawl. Time had bent her back, softened her voice, but her eyes — they still held that fierce warmth. She wept silently. Not out of sadness. But because she'd seen too many stories that ended in goodbyes. Ours was a rare hello that stayed.

I wore a plain white kurta. The cloth was simple, like my past. But the way I stood — shoulders back, heart full — I felt like the richest man alive.

Rani… she wore a cream saree, modest and soft. And in her hair, tucked like a promise, was that red ribbon — the same one she once tied to my wrist when we were children, hoping it would bring me strength.

There was no priest. No heavy chants. No stage lit by chandeliers. Just us. Under an open sky. Bare-hearted. Bare-souled.

I took her hand, looked into her eyes and said:

"I was once a boy who begged — not just for food, but for love, for hope… for a reason to wake up. You were the first person who gave me all three… without ever asking for anything in return."

Her eyes shimmered as she replied:

"And I was a girl who had stopped believing in miracles — until I saw God in the eyes of a stranger on a street corner. You didn't need saving, Deepak. You just needed someone to believe in your magic. And I did. I always did."

There was silence after that — not awkward, but sacred. Even the stars seemed to lean in closer.

We weren't married in a marble hall, but beneath a sky stitched with moonlight and memories.

We didn't have chandeliers — just stars.

No shehnais — just the wind, the rustle of leaves and the giggles of children who once called the streets home.

And in that moment — in that one wild, beautiful moment — it wasn't just a wedding.

It was the building of a home.

Not with bricks.

But with **belonging**.

Chapter 34 : A House Made of Hopes

Our first home wasn't grand. In fact, most people would've walked right past it without a second glance. A one-bedroom flat tucked into the far end of a tired old building, its walls weathered, its staircase creaky, its lift always "under maintenance."

But to us — to me and Rani — it was a palace.

Not because of what it had. But because of what it meant.

The kitchen was tiny. Yet every morning, it hissed to life as Rani brewed chai, humming softly under her breath. The balcony was barely big enough for two, but each sunrise that tiptoed in felt like a quiet miracle just for us. The walls still smelled of fresh paint, but beneath that — if you stood still, really still — you could breathe in something far deeper.

New beginnings.

We had no luxuries. The furniture was borrowed, donated or rescued from street corners and flea markets. A wobbly dining table. A fan that groaned more than it spun. A sofa that dipped to one side like it had carried too many stories. And yet… we loved it all.

Because every crack was part of our journey. Every scuff on the wall had laughter echoing behind it.

Sundays were our favourite — the radio would play old Hindi songs, the aroma of haldi and roasted jeera would fill the air and we'd slow dance between cooking and chores. Our chai cups never stayed full — not because we lacked, but because the talking always came first and the chai was just an excuse.

Rani brought magic into that home.

She made curtains out of her old sarees — each patch sewn by hand, each thread whispering a piece of our past. She planted succulents in chipped mugs and gave them names like *Umeed* and *Muskaan.* She turned forgotten corners into cozy nooks, framed dried flowers in her journals and turned discarded keys and seashells into a wind chime that sang every time the breeze visited.

And me? I was working at a small grassroots startup, helping street kids find purpose. Not a fancy job — but a full one. Every boy I mentored reminded me of the boy I used to be. Lost. Hungry — not for food, but for belief. Giving back wasn't charity. It was my way of thanking the universe for Rani. For a second chance. For breath.

Our home wasn't built with cement and paint. It was built with held hands, hushed prayers and stitched-together dreams.

Yes, the bathroom tap leaked now and then. And the doorbell… well, it had a personality of its own — sometimes ringing even when no one was outside. But we laughed. We joked, "Our house might not be perfect, but it gives us perfect reasons to come back."

Most nights, we'd sit on the balcony floor, feet dangling, chai growing cold between our palms, watching the city shimmer — this same city that once turned its back on us. But from up here, with her by my side, I didn't feel angry anymore.
Just… peaceful.

We used to joke that our home didn't hold wealth — it leaked love. Love that slipped through our cracked walls and danced into the world outside.

It wasn't just a shelter. It was proof — quiet, stubborn, radiant proof — that broken things can still build **something beautiful**.

Chapter 35 : Building More Than Walls

Every Sunday morning, while the city still stretched and yawned its way into the day, Rani and I would lace up our worn-out shoes and walk — hand in hand — to the same traffic signal where once upon a time, our lives had collided.

The same spot where I had begged with a tin can and tired eyes.

The same spot where she had once looked at me — not with pity, but with purpose.

But we didn't return there as beggars anymore.

We went back as givers.

What we had started was small. Quiet. Almost invisible in the noise of the world. But it burned with purpose. A weekend school — not in name, but in spirit — for street children. For those who slept under plastic sheets. Who sold roses and balloons at red lights with hands too small and eyes too old. Who learned to count coins long before they ever held a pencil.

We called it **Aangan**.

Not a school. Not an institution.

Just... *Aangan* — a courtyard.

A place where stories begin.

Where you're not questioned about your past, but nurtured for your future.

We didn't have buildings or benches. We had pavement corners, chalk-drawn circles, trees that shaded our lessons and cardboard boxes turned into blackboards.

But what we gave them was something no textbook could hold: *belonging*.

Rani had this way of turning every class into magic.

She’d tell stories that turned beggar kids into brave kings and clever queens. She'd make them paint — wildly, freely — on discarded cardboard with crooked brushes and even crookeder smiles. They’d dance barefoot, offbeat and untamed, not to learn technique, but to feel what joy tastes like when it’s your own.

I handled the quieter parts.

I taught them English — broken, like mine once was — but with love stitched between every syllable. I taught them about savings with pebbles and tin boxes and how to introduce themselves with pride. Most of all, I tried to teach them what I had never been taught:

That you are more than where you come from.

That you can write your name in the world, not just in dust.

Soon enough, they stopped calling us *Sir* and *Ma’am*.

Those names felt too far, too polished, too unfamiliar.

They called us *Bhaiya. Didi.*

And the littlest ones — the ones who still stammered on long words — just called us *Home*.
One day, a boy with a runny nose and the kind of eyes that had already seen too much asked Rani, “Didi, are you and Bhaiya magicians?”

She smiled, brushing his hair back. “Why do you say that?”

He looked down, shrugged, then said softly,

"Because… when you come here, it doesn't feel like a street anymore. It feels like my mother might come find me here. Or like I could become someone… someone big."

Rani didn't reply. She just hugged him.

And in that moment, I think we both believed in magic too.

We never handed out certificates. We had no government support, no NGO status, no donors lining up.

But every Sunday, more children came back.

Barefoot. Wide-eyed. Some shy. Some carrying baby siblings. All carrying hope like a secret treasure buried deep inside.

And on those chaotic mornings, with crayons scattered, songs sung off-key and chalk dust clinging to our clothes, I would look at Rani and whisper, "We thought we were building a school."

She'd smile and say, "But we're building lives."

Because the truest walls aren't made of bricks and cement.

They're built from trust. From love. From the raw, relentless belief that even the most broken beginnings can still grow into **something meaningful.**

Chapter 36 : The Tiny Miracle

The years had tiptoed by — softly, gently — like old friends walking through a room filled with fragile memories. Life had become quieter. Steadier. Not perfect, no… but deeply ours. The chaos we once survived now hummed like a lullaby in the background — a soft reminder that peace, when earned, sings sweeter.

One crisp morning, as the city outside yawned into motion, Rani left a small, folded note beside my cup of chai. It was shaped like a paper boat — clumsy, uneven — just like the ones we used to float in monsoon puddles as kids.

Still half-asleep, I unfolded it.

In her messy, slanted handwriting, it said:

"I think there's going to be a new story in our house soon…"

I stared at it, confused.

Then she appeared from the kitchen, barefoot and glowing — her eyes glinting with mischief and something even more beautiful: hope. From behind her back, she pulled out a pair of the tiniest white crocheted booties I had ever seen.

She held them like they were sacred.

It took me a second to understand. Maybe two.

Then the breath left my chest like someone had opened a window to my soul.

And the tears came. Not the heavy ones I'd once cried under streetlights, wrapped in hunger and shame — but the kind that spill quietly, like blessings you never had the courage to ask for.

I pulled her into my arms, speechless. The paper boat slipped from my fingers and floated gently to the floor, but its message had already found its place — docked forever in the harbour of our hearts.

The next nine months passed like a sacred countdown.

Morning sickness. Midnight cravings. Belly lullabies. Soft hands on stretched skin. Every kick felt like a secret knock from the other side of the stars. We built a cradle — not just of wood and nails, but of memories, fears, whispered prayers and a love we had once thought life had denied us forever.

And then, on a rain-washed monsoon morning, the sky split with thunder — like the universe clearing its throat to make an announcement.

He arrived.

Our son.

Red-faced. Pink-skinned. Crying like he was writing his first poem in the air. The rain tapped gently on the hospital window and somewhere in the distance, a temple bell chimed — as if even the gods had paused to welcome him.

I stood frozen as the nurse placed him in my arms.

Swaddled in white, with tiny fists curled like commas and eyes barely open, he looked like he had fallen straight from a storybook. Or maybe heaven.

My hands shook.

And in that single moment, every scar on my soul — every night on cold pavement, every rejection, every ache — vanished.
There was only *this*.

This heartbeat.

This warmth.

This impossible, beautiful proof that broken people can still build miracles.

We named him **Akash** — sky — because he was born to rise. To be free. To hold everything we once thought we'd lost.

Later that night, in the hush of our hospital room, Rani held him close, kissed his forehead and whispered:

"He's our full circle."

And he was.

Life shifted — in all the right ways.

The nights became lullabies sung half-awake, arms cradling dreams wrapped in diapers and soft blankets. Our living room, once quiet and sparse, exploded into colour — stuffed toys, rattles, burp cloths and laughter that danced like wind chimes caught in summer breeze.
Rani glowed differently now. Tired but luminous. Humming lullabies even when she slept.

And I… I would often stand in the doorway at 3 a.m., watching her rock Akash gently, the nightlight painting halos around them both.

And I'd think:

From a boy who once begged for love on the streets…

To a man holding the whole sky in his arms. How did I get this lucky?

Chapter 37 : Good Bye Laxmi Aunty

One rainy evening, as the sky wept quietly, I received a message that sent chills down my spine. An old beggar from our past, someone I barely remembered, found me on the streets and whispered,
"Laxmi Aunty… she's dying. She's asking for you."

For a moment, the world paused. It had been years since I'd seen her—since I'd escaped the world she'd built around me like a cage. I didn't know how to feel. She was the woman who raised me, who taught me to beg, who hurt me, fed me, scolded me and in her own twisted way, protected me.

The next morning, I went to see her. The air in the small room was heavy with the smell of incense and illness. She lay on a worn-out mattress, her body now just a shadow of the fierce woman I once feared. Her eyes were closed, but the moment she heard my footsteps, they fluttered open. They were weak, but they still held a strange fire.

"Deepak…" she murmured, her voice dry and cracking. "You came."

I sat beside her, unsure of what to say. She reached for my hand with trembling fingers and looked at me—not as the boy she once punished, but almost like a mother seeing her child one last time.

"I don't have long," she whispered. "And there's something I must tell you… something you have the right to know."

I didn't breathe. I just listened.

"I didn't find you in a basket. I didn't pick you up from a temple gate like I told others… I bought you." Her voice broke, but she continued. "I bought you from a man in Delhi's Nizamuddin slum… for fifty thousand rupees."

I stared at her, stunned. The walls of the room seemed to tilt. My fingers dug into the sides of the mattress.

"He said he'd found you… that he stole you from Sanjeevani Hospital. You were just a few days old. I didn't ask much. I just… I wanted a baby I could raise for my work." She closed her eyes, a tear sliding down the creases of her cheek. "I was selfish."

I couldn't speak. My throat was dry. The room spun and in it, I saw flashes—of the child I was, crying in the sun at traffic signals, wearing tattered clothes, being handed off like a prop. And now, in the dim light of this room, I found out I wasn't even hers. I wasn't even abandoned. I was *taken.*

The tears came like a flood—silent, heavy, raw. I wasn't crying for her. I was crying for the child I had been. For the parents who had lost me. For the years spent not knowing who I truly was.

"I'm sorry," she said. "I don't know if it matters anymore… but I needed you to know the truth."

I stood there for a while, holding her hand, both of us lost in the silence between the living and the dying. I didn't hate her anymore. I had grown past hate. But the pain… the pain would take longer to leave.

That night, Laxmi Aunty passed away. Quietly. Alone.

And I left with a piece of truth I never knew I was missing.

Chapter 38 : In Search for My Roots

The night after Laxmi Aunty died, I couldn't sleep. Her final words kept echoing in my ears: *"He stole you from Sanjeevani Hospital."*

For so many years, I thought I was just an unlucky child, left behind by fate. But now I knew—I wasn't abandoned. I was *stolen*.

For the first time in my life, I had a name. *Sanjeevani Hospital, Delhi.* That was where I had come into this world. Maybe, just maybe, someone had been looking for me all these years. My real parents… my real name… my real beginning.

I sat on the balcony of our small home, Akash asleep inside, his tiny snores reminding me of how much life had changed. Rani came out, sat beside me and placed her hand gently over mine. She could feel the storm inside me before I even spoke.

"She bought me, Rani," I whispered, eyes still on the sky. "I wasn't an orphan. I was taken."

Rani didn't say anything right away. She just leaned her head on my shoulder. "What do you want to do?" she finally asked.

"I want to find them. I want to know who I am. I owe that to myself… and to Akash. I don't want him to grow up not knowing his roots."

Rani replied "So began the search."

The next few weeks were a blur of train rides between Mumbai and Delhi, old file requests and long hours at police stations and hospitals in Delhi. I was chasing a ghost—a crime that was committed more than two decades ago. At Sanjeevani Hospital, most of the old staff was gone, the records were dusty, some lost, some eaten by time. But then… one nurse remembered.

“I was there that week,” she said softly, her eyes scanning my face.

“There was a couple… they had a baby boy who disappeared from the main entrance gate of the hospital after they got discharged. I remember it clearly. The mother had fainted from shock.”

My heart stopped. *That could be me.*

I gave a DNA sample to the missing persons cell and they promised to cross-match it with old cases still open in their database.

The wait was brutal. Days felt like months.

Back home, I tried to act normal, but every time Akash called me *papa*, I felt like a stranger to myself. How could I teach him about life when I didn’t even know where mine had started?

One afternoon, while feeding Akash his lunch, the call came. The officer on the other end said just one word:

“We found a match.”

Chapter 39 : The Face That Looked Like Mine

When I reached Delhi again, this time I wasn't just looking for clues—I was going to meet *them*. My real parents.

The officer who called me had arranged the meeting at the police station. He said it was safer, more contained. I understood. After all, for them, this would be a storm too. A child lost twenty-five years ago… suddenly standing at their door.

As I walked into the small waiting room, my heart pounded so hard it echoed in my ears. I kept my eyes down, afraid of building expectations. What if they didn't want me? What if they'd moved on?

Then I heard a soft gasp.

I looked up… and saw her.

She was wearing a pale yellow saree, her eyes sunken but shining, lips trembling as if caught between a prayer and a cry. And next to her was a man—tall, with streaks of grey in his hair and hands shaking just slightly as he clutched a photograph. My photograph. From when I was a baby.

They stood slowly. The woman took a step forward, then another, then stopped. Her hand was over her mouth now. The man looked at me as if staring into a mirror from the past.

Then she whispered:

"Beta?"

That word—just four letters—broke something inside me. I hadn't known my name. I didn't even know *they* remembered.

Tears poured down my face and I nodded.

She ran to me and wrapped her arms around me like she'd been holding that hug in for twenty-five years. I could feel her body trembling against mine. The man—my *father*—placed his hand on my shoulder and for the first time in my life, I felt what a father's touch meant. Firm. Protective. Silent with strength.

They were Dr. Sameer and Dr. Kavita Sharma. Both had been young doctors at the time of my birth, working at Sanjeevani Hospital. They had left me alone in the car for just a few minutes while my mother fainted right at the doorstep because of weakness and in that small moment, their world had collapsed. The CCTV wasn't working. The security guard had vanished. And so had I.

"I thought I lost you forever," my mother cried, holding my face in both hands. "I thought God had punished us."

I told them about Laxmi Aunty, about the streets, about begging, about Rani and Akash. And they cried, not just for what I'd suffered—but also for the life I had built despite it.

Then my father did something unexpected—he stood up, wiped his tears and said:

"You are stronger than all of us, son. You've lived ten lives in one. We can't take away what happened… but from today, you don't have to carry it alone anymore."

We sat together for hours, just sharing stories, photos and silences that needed no words.

When I finally left Delhi to return to Rani and Akash, I wasn't empty anymore. I wasn't lost.

I had roots now. A name. A past. And also, a future.

Chapter 40 : When Two Worlds Met

The train ride back from Delhi was different this time. It wasn't heavy with questions or haunted by shadows. Instead, it carried something fragile—hope. A new kind of nervousness filled me. How would Rani react? How would I tell Akash that his grandparents were alive and searching for me all these years?

When I reached home, the sun had already dipped behind the buildings. Rani opened the door with her usual smile, but her eyes immediately read my face.

"Something happened," she said softly, brushing the dust off my shoulder like it mattered. "You found them… didn't you?"

I nodded.

And then, without waiting, she pulled me in, sat me down and said, "Tell me everything."

So I did.

I told her about Dr. Sameer and Dr. Kavita. About the photograph. About my real name. About the moment my mother hugged me, saying *"Deepu"*, like she'd held that name in her mouth for decades, waiting to breathe it again. I told her about the warmth, the shock, the tears. I told her how they had never stopped looking.

By the end, she was crying too. But not in pain. In peace. "I'm happy for you, Deepak," she whispered, holding my hand. "Truly. Your story finally found its missing piece."

Then I looked at Akash, who had been listening quietly from the doorway. I knelt down and said, "Beta, your Dada and Dadi are in Delhi. They've been looking for Papa since I was… even smaller than you."

He blinked, surprised and smiled by looking at Deepak's face. He was too small to understand this. We planned the visit a few days later. Not just me this time—but all three of us.

The moment we stepped into my parents' house, Rani's hand tightened around mine. It was a large home, filled with things we'd never known: polished wood, family portraits, fresh flowers in every corner. But it wasn't the luxury that struck us—it was the warmth.

Kavita rushed forward, eyes on Akash first. "This must be him," she whispered, kneeling down.

Akash looked at me for confirmation. I smiled and nodded. She opened her arms. "Can I hug you?"

Akash took a moment… then walked into her arms like it was always meant to be.

Sameer shook hands with Rani, holding her gaze for a second longer than usual. "Thank you," he said. "For walking with him through everything."

Rani replied with a smile, "I'd do it all over again."

That day, two families—one born from blood, the other built through survival—sat at one table, sharing food, memories and laughter. No one asked for forgiveness. No one blamed fate. We just… accepted.

Later that evening, Kavita brought out a tiny baby sweater. "I had knit this for you, Deepu," she said. "I couldn't give it then. But maybe… maybe you'd like to keep it now?"

I took it in my hands, heart trembling. It was proof. Not just of where I'd come from—but of how deeply I had always been loved, even when I didn't know it.

Chapter 41 : The House That Healed Us

The Delhi bungalow wasn't just a place I stayed in—it was a living, breathing presence that met me when I had nothing left but broken pieces. It didn't speak, but I swear it listened. It listened to the weariness in our footsteps, the trembling in our voices, the weight of all we had carried for so long. It was the first place that didn't demand anything from me. It just… let me be.

The lane was quiet, lined with Gulmohar trees that dropped orange-red petals like little blessings. The house stood with its whitewashed walls and ivy clinging to its sides like old memories that refused to leave. Every morning, light poured in as if the sun itself wanted to enter gently, respectfully. The verandas stretched out like arms, offering a kind of warmth I didn't know a building could offer. The windows didn't just open to the street—they opened to a second chance. Inside, everything whispered peace. The cushions didn't show off, but when I sat on them, they seemed to say, *"It's okay. You're safe now."* The curtains swayed with the breeze like forgiving hands, brushing away years of pain. Even the cool floors under my feet grounded me—as if saying, *"You're here. You made it."*

There was space for everyone. But no room ever felt cold or distant. The house didn't echo—it absorbed. It held silence without letting it become loneliness. It allowed room for grief to sit beside us, quietly, without needing to explain itself. There was a corner for every unsaid story, every stifled sob, every dream we had once buried.

For the first time, I began to understand what people meant when they said *home*. Not a roof over your head, not just walls and doors. *Home* was this: a place that accepts all of you, even the parts you're ashamed of. A place that lets your past sit beside your present without fighting.

Mornings here were different. There were no angry horns or footsteps rushing past you. Just the gentle hum of filter coffee from the kitchen and birdsong that felt like it was singing *to us*. I would sit on the front veranda with Dr. Sameer—my father—and we would sip chai in silence. Not the uncomfortable kind, but the kind that holds you together. Sometimes we talked about cricket, politics, clouds… sometimes nothing at all. And yet, I felt something shifting between us—an invisible string being retied, one cup, one silence at a time. One evening, without thinking, I leaned my head on his shoulder. No words were spoken. None were needed. That small gesture said everything we hadn't been able to for years.

Rani… she blossomed. That house gave her roots. Every morning, she brought home fresh marigolds or jasmine from the market and placed them on the table like offerings of joy. She rearranged the kitchen not out of necessity, but out of love. For the first time, she wasn't a shadow. She was seen. Admired. She wasn't surviving—she was living.

Kavita—my mother—taught her how to make pasta, garlic bread, even soup from scratch. She encouraged Rani to read again. And she did—romantic novels, poetry, stories with happy endings she had never dared to dream for herself. Her laughter changed. It wasn't sharp or nervous anymore—it was warm, round, full. She hummed while folding clothes, while feeding Akash. Sometimes, when the world was quiet, we'd sneak away to the nearby park and sit beneath the Champa tree, just the two of us. We spoke about nothing. We spoke about everything. How strange it felt to be safe. How terrifying it was to imagine losing it.

That house didn't erase our pain. It didn't wave a wand and fix us. But it gave us the space to breathe, to speak, to cry, to rest. It made healing feel possible. Slowly, we began to believe that scars could live beside joy. That we could carry our wounds without being defined by them. It wasn't just a house. It was **our resurrection**.

Chapter 42 : Dr. Sameer and Dr. Kavita - Parents Reclaimed

They hadn't just been waiting to find me. They were waiting to find *themselves* again—as parents. And when that moment finally came, it wasn't loud or dramatic. It didn't arrive with teary reunions or grand gestures. It came quietly—fragile, unsure—like broken pieces testing if they could still fit.

I could feel the guilt in them, even when they didn't speak of it. Not the kind that fades over time, but the kind that lingers beneath smiles. It sat with us at the breakfast table, followed us during evening walks. Guilt that they hadn't been there when I cried through fevers, hadn't sung me to sleep, hadn't clapped during my birthdays or sang birthday songs. They hadn't seen my first steps. Or my hundredth fall. Someone else had lived those moments with me. And that truth… I could see how deeply it haunted them.

But despite that sorrow, they never let guilt poison the gift of *now*. Every moment we shared felt like something they unwrapped with trembling hands—carefully, gratefully. They didn't ask me to call them *Ma* or *Papa*. They didn't need grand expressions of love. They just… showed up. Gently. Consistently.

Dr. Sameer—my father—was known for his calm, commanding presence during his hospital days. But with me, on the veranda, he became someone softer. He never lectured. He listened. Not like a man chasing lost years, but like a father just trying to know his son—who I was beneath the grime of my story. And he never pitied me. He respected me. For surviving. For not letting bitterness consume me. For holding on to integrity when I had every reason not to.

One evening, as the sky turned orange, he turned to me and said, "I couldn't keep you safe, Deepak… but someone else did. And for that, I will be grateful all my life."

He meant Laxmi Aunty. And when I showed him a photo of her—just a grainy image on my phone—he printed it, framed it and placed it quietly on a shelf in his study. No words. Just a silent bow to the woman who had held me when they couldn't.

And then there was *her*—Dr. Kavita. My mother. She didn't walk into Rani's life like a mother-in-law. She walked in like someone who had found a missing part of herself. From the first day, there was no stiffness between them. She never talked *down* to Rani, never offered advice wrapped in judgment. She treated her like an equal. Like a woman she respected. Like family.

They bonded over kitchen chaos, over flower markets and spice jars. But more than that, they bonded through vulnerability. Kavita Ma shared stories she hadn't told anyone in years—how she'd cried herself to sleep the first few months of marriage, how loneliness had crept in even when she was surrounded by people. Her honesty surprised us. It opened a quiet door in Rani's heart.

She taught Rani how to fold a sari with grace, how to smell a mango and know if it's ripe, how to calm a crying child with nothing but warm oil and loving hands. But she never made Rani feel small. She watched her closely, mothering Akash with love and fear in equal parts and only stepped in when asked. One afternoon, while Rani was folding Akash's clothes in the courtyard, Kavita Ma brought out a small silver anklet. Worn. Beautiful. From her own childhood. "For him," she said, placing it in Rani's palm. Then she paused and added gently, "And for you. Because you're part of us now."

It was a simple gesture. No speeches. No declarations. Just love, offered in quiet ways—a cup of tea at dusk, a new recipe tried together, lullabies hummed side-by-side in the nursery. They didn't try to erase the past. They didn't try to start over. They reclaimed their place in our lives—not by force, but with love. And somehow, in doing that… **we all found home**.

Chapter 43 : Akash - The Joy They Never Knew They Missed

If I was the missing piece in their story, then Akash was the golden thread that stitched us all together—softly, brightly, beautifully. He didn't just arrive in our lives. He *transformed* them. His giggles filled spaces where sorrow had once sat quietly. His tiny, curious hands reached into places we didn't even know were still aching—and without trying, he healed them.

When he toddled through the corridors of the Delhi bungalow, it was like the house forgot it had ever been heavy with grief. Those cold marble floors, once silent witnesses to pain, now echoed with the music of little feet, of joy in motion. He brought the walls to life. The house didn't just feel full—it felt *reborn*.

I often watched Ma—Dr. Kavita—at night as she sat by Akash's bed. Her fingers moved gently through his hair as she told him bedtime stories. But those weren't just stories. They were whispers from a past she had never lived—the tales she had imagined telling *me* once upon a time. About brave monkeys and clever crows and magical trees. Every word she spoke wove love into Akash's dreams—and slowly, into her own healing. I could see it: the peace returning to her eyes, like a long-lost friend finally knocking at the door.

And Papa—Dr. Sameer—my stoic, composed father… he changed too. People knew him as a man who could face the gravest of emergencies without blinking. But now I saw him lying flat on the living room floor, surrounded by gems (jelly beans) and coins, teaching Akash to count.

Akash would respond with a squeal and a wordless string of baby-talk that somehow made perfect sense to all of us. It wasn't just play. It was time reclaimed. A language of love that didn't need grammar.

Akash was endlessly curious. No sound escaped his questions. No ritual went unnoticed. He examined everything with wide-eyed wonder—from how the pressure cooker hissed to why Papa wore a his shoes. The house bore his fingerprints, his spirit. Crayon drawings taped to the fridge. Toys scattered across the hall like sacred offerings. Little muddy shoes lined up near the door, waiting for tomorrow's adventure. The once-silent bungalow now throbbed with laughter, mischief and movement.

But more than anything, Akash was proof—living, breathing proof—that broken stories can still bloom. That loss doesn't always mean the end. That love, when it returns, often does so in new shapes—smaller hands, brighter eyes, louder joy.

He didn't just complete our family.

He brought us **back to life**.

Chapter 44 : Small Moments, Deep Roots

Not every day brought a miracle. There were no grand revelations, no dramatic turns. And oddly enough—that was the most miraculous part.

Because the magic was hiding in the ordinary.

It lived in the way our mornings began with filter coffee and the rustle of newspapers, in the way Rani braided Akash's hair just a little differently each day, in how Ma folded fresh clothes still warm from the sun. It was stitched into the pauses, into the laughter, into the rituals that built themselves quietly—until one day, they became *life*.

I remember one warm afternoon in the backyard. I was planting a sapling, elbows deep in soft earth, when Rani came and knelt beside me. She pushed her dupatta behind her ears and helped me press the soil down around the roots. Our fingers touched—muddy, clumsy, human.

"Let's call it *Hope*," I whispered.

Not to make a statement. Not for drama. Just… as a prayer. It wasn't just a plant. It was a piece of what we were growing together. New soil. New roots. A new shot at everything.

Our lives started blooming in the smallest of ways.

Birthdays became our own strange, sacred celebrations. Cakes were always uneven. Rani baked them, Ma frosted them with more love than technique. Songs were off-key and sung with all the wrong words—but Akash squealed with delight every single time. Candles were never just his to blow. Everyone leaned in, laughing, helping him wish.

Sundays were for family—walks in Lodhi Garden, ice creams from cycle vendors, rickshaw rides that left us windblown and alive. One evening at India Gate, Akash wandered off for just five minutes—but for Ma, it was five lifetimes. When we found him clutching a balloon near a peanut seller, she dropped to her knees and held him like she might disappear too.

"I thought… I lost him too," she whispered. And we all knew *exactly* what she meant.

That Diwali—it wasn't a festival. It was a revelation.

The house shimmered under the glow of dozens of diyas. Every flicker seemed to pulse with memory. Rangolis were messy but vibrant. Sparklers lit up our faces—not as signs of wealth, but of reunion. Of survival. Of having made it, against all odds.

In the corner of the puja room, nestled between framed deities and jasmine garlands, sat a photograph of Laxmi Aunty. Her eyes kind. Her smile captured in time. We placed marigolds by her photo every day leading up to Diwali—not just on the day. A quiet act. No announcements. No speeches.

It was Ma's idea.

"She gave him life," she said, her voice clear. "I gave him birth. We're both his mothers."

She didn't say it with bitterness. There was no competition in her tone. Only grace. Only truth. And in that moment, I understood what family really meant. It wasn't just blood. It was love. Sacrifice. And second chances.

Our evenings were delightfully unremarkable. Dinner was usually noisy—someone always spilled the dal. Akash chattered in rhymes. Rani hummed while folding laundry. I'd help Ma string jasmine flowers for the puja. And Papa? He'd fall asleep with his glasses slipping and a novel open like a blanket over his chest.

But under those small, repeating acts, something larger was taking root.

A forest was growing.

Deep, tangled, invisible roots of belonging. Of safety. Of a love that didn't need to prove anything anymore.

We weren't just *living*.

We were *healing*.

Chapter 45 : The Pull of Purpose

Delhi had become my comfort. A quiet rhythm of warm meals, safe nights and familiar laughter. For the first time in years, I had a pillow that smelled like home, not sweat and concrete. A son who giggled in his sleep. A wife who sang while folding clothes. Parents who had finally become real, not just names on a lost file.

But even peace has its own restlessness.

It wasn't unhappiness—I wasn't running from anything. I was being pulled.

There was this silent tug I couldn't ignore. A soft, persistent throb deep in my chest. Like an old song trying to return to its chorus. It wasn't ambition. It was something older, deeper. A *purpose.*

Every night, after Akash fell asleep—his belly full, cheeks warm, a soft blanket tucked up to his chin—I'd sit beside him and just *watch.* And without fail, my mind would slip to another child.

A boy just like him, but sleeping under a torn tarpaulin. The sound of passing trains rattling his bones. A girl crouched by a traffic light, hand out, eyes blank. A child whose name would never be written on a school form, whose birthday no one remembered, whose smile had dried up from too much sun and too little love.

I couldn't unsee them. One evening, I turned to Rani, my fingers brushing gently through Akash's hair. I didn't mean to speak, but the words came anyway.

"There are so many Akashs out there…" I said, barely above a whisper. "So many who'll never be this warm. Who'll never be *called* someone's son."

Rani didn't flinch. Didn't ask questions. She simply placed her hand over mine. Her grip steady. Her voice steady too.

"Then maybe… it's time." That's all she said. And somehow, that one sentence held everything—permission, support, faith.

A few days later, I sat with Papa on the veranda. The air carried a slight chill and the scent of jasmine drifted in from the garden. Dusk softened the city into a watercolour blur.

"I think I want to go back," I said. My voice didn't shake. "To Mumbai. To the streets I came from. I want to start something. A shelter. A school. A platform. Something for kids like me—kids with no voice, no name, no chance. Someone has to speak for them… someone who *was* them."

He didn't speak for a while. He didn't need to. Papa just listened, like he always had—like a man who knew the sacred weight of a calling. Then, finally, he placed his hand on my shoulder. Firm. Warm.

"The world needs your voice," he said. "You were born in pain, Deepak. But raised in purpose. You carry both. And that's rare. Go where your fire takes you. We'll always be here."

I nodded, eyes burning, heart calm. That moment wasn't a goodbye. It was an unlocking. A turning of the page. My story in that peaceful house didn't end. It *prepared* me.

Together—with Rani, with Ma and Papa—we began planning. Mapping out ideas. Making calls. Listing what we had and what we'd need.

Not because I was leaving them behind. But because I had finally found the reason I had survived it all.

Chapter 46 : The Vanishing of Akash

Nine months. That's how long we had been living in Delhi—me, Rani and our little Akash. In those nine months, the scars had softened. Our days had found rhythm. Mornings started with birdsong and the clink of Ma's bangles. Evenings ended with Papa pretending to fall asleep mid-story while Akash giggled uncontrollably.

That morning felt no different.

The sun was gentle, the earth still smelled of last night's rain and Akash's laughter filled the air as he played outside with the neighbourhood kids. Rani was in the kitchen, humming an old tune, stirring dal like it was an offering to the gods. I was on the dining table, flipping through notes for a small event I was scheduled to speak at—my story, my survival, my purpose.

It was peaceful. Simple.

Until it wasn't.

The silence came first. Sudden. Thick. That kind of silence that presses down on your chest before something terrible happens—like the world itself holding its breath.

"Akash! Lunch is ready!" Rani called out standing at the main entrance of our house. No answer.

She called again, louder. Still nothing.

Something inside me shifted. A chill. A knot. I looked up and our eyes met—and in that instant, we both knew something wasn't right.

I dropped the papers and ran out.

The kids were still there, their faces confused, unsure.

"Uncle…" one of them said, voice trembling, "a man came in a white car. He said he was Akash's uncle. He gave him chocolate… and then… he took him."

Took him.

The words didn't make sense. They didn't *register*. They just echoed. Took him.

My knees buckled for a second. I turned and Rani was already there. She looked at the empty space where Akash should've been and then she screamed.

Not a cry. Not a wail. A scream that tore through the sky. A scream only a mother can make.

We called the police. Filed the report. Showed them pictures. His yellow T-shirt with the cartoon lion. His tiny blue sandals. His missing tooth. His laugh. His name. Everything.

Neighbours gathered. Some whispered. Some cried. Some offered prayers. Others pointed fingers. But nothing mattered.

Our son was gone.

That night, I sat on the cold floor of our bedroom, holding the little sweater Ma had once knit for me as a baby—the same one she had saved all these years, the same one Akash now wore when it got chilly. I pressed it to my face, breathing in the faint smell of powder, mango candy and innocence.

And then something inside me cracked open.

This had happened before.

A child taken.

A life stolen.

Me.

I had lived this nightmare once—from the other side. And now it had come for *my* child.

But I wasn't that boy anymore.

I wasn't lost. Or voiceless. Or powerless.

This time, I wasn't wearing rags. I wasn't begging for scraps.

This time, I was a father.

A father with fire in his bones and fury in his blood.

And if I had to tear down every lie, every locked door, every goddamn evil that stole children from their names and homes—I would.

Because this time, I wasn't going to be rescued.

This time, I was going to rescue *him*.

Chapter 47 : Back to the City That Took Me

I never imagined I'd return to Delhi—not like this.

This was the city that gave me life and then swallowed me whole. The city of my disappearance. The city where I became no one. And now, years later, it had reached out its hand and stolen my son.

Within hours of Akash's kidnapping, I knew what I had to do. I packed a bag I never looked at twice, held Rani longer than I should've and left her behind with Ma and Papa. Her fingers tightened around mine, her voice cracking as she said, "Bring him back."

"I will," I promised. I didn't know how. But I had to.

Delhi hadn't changed. Or maybe it had and I'd just grown too far from its rhythm to notice.

The scent of roasted peanuts still danced at corners. Rickshaws still raced like they were dodging fate. Street vendors still shouted over one another like the louder one might rewrite history. But this time, I wasn't the boy in rags, clinging to strangers.

I was the man they'd stolen from.

I retraced every shadow of my childhood—

Sanjeevani Hospital, where the timeline of my life had been split in two.

The slums where children chased tyres barefoot.

The train station where tiny bodies still curled against concrete like forgotten notes in a song no one sang anymore.

I spoke to anyone who would look me in the eye.

Chaiwalas. Rickshaw pullers. Ragpickers. Beggars. Old women who watched the world from broken stools.

I showed them Akash's photo. A grainy print from my phone. His smile wide, his cap red.

Most shook their heads. A few took the paper gently, stared at it too long and then said nothing at all.

I visited NGOs. Police stations. Shelters. Sat across tables with officers trained to be numb. Some offered sympathy. Others, impatience. One even said, "Sir, thousands go missing every month. Try to stay hopeful."

Stay hopeful?

A week passed. Then another.

My beard grew, unshaped. My voice turned rough from repeating the same lines. My hands stopped trembling, but only because they'd grown too used to holding despair.

One night, I stood beneath the same old streetlamp near Sanjeevani Hospital—flickering like it too had lost faith—and held the last photo of Akash.

And I whispered to no one,

"Is this how my parents felt the day I vanished?"

The grief hit me like a delayed punch.

I remembered Laxmi Aunt's last confession—how she bought me for ₹50,000 from a man right here. I'd buried that memory. But now, it clawed its way back.

What if it wasn't just the same city?

What if it was the same network? The same faces in new names?

But the man she spoke of was gone—dead or invisible.

So I kept searching.

Every time a child knocked on a window at a red light, I looked too hard. Each small frame became a maybe. Each passing second became a prayer.

But Akash was in none of them.

So I started going farther—Gurgaon, Noida, Ghaziabad.

I followed whispers. Called fake leads. Slept in lodges with peeling walls and slow fans. I'd lie awake, holding the red cap I'd found at home—his favourite. It still smelled of talcum powder and sunshine.
That night, the tears didn't scream. They just… fell.

I was the boy who'd been lost. Now a father, searching for the son who had vanished.

But this time, the streets didn't speak.

This time, the city had shut its doors and swallowed its answers.

And I—

I was unravelling.

Chapter 48 : 100 Questions, No Answer

How does a father survive when the world goes quiet?

Not peaceful quiet—no.

This was the silence of absence. Of dread. Of a scream that's been swallowed.

Each morning, I woke up with a new plan.

A new rumour.

A new sliver of madness that dressed itself as hope.

Today, I'd tell myself. Today, I'll find him.

Today, he'll run into my arms, breathless, muddy, still wearing that mischievous smile.

And he'll ask, "Papa, what took you so long?"

But every evening ended the same.

With my legs trembling.

My voice cracked from repeating the same questions to people who didn't care.

My mind spiralling like a moth in a glass jar.

And my heart—always my heart—waiting on that same rusted bench in Central Park, breaking over and over again.

The red cap he wore the day he vanished… it's still in my pocket.

Frayed now. Faded.

The last piece of him that still listens when I speak.

I asked everyone:

"Did anyone see a boy taken from Neel Nagar that evening?"

Strangers shook their heads.

Some walked away mid-sentence.

Some stared at me like I was mad.

And I kept asking.

"Was he crying?"

"Was someone watching us all this time?"

"Did he call out for me until his voice gave out?"

Questions.

Only questions.

And no one answering.

I returned to the train station where my own story had lost its path.

I stood amidst the same chaos.

Children still wandered with sunburnt skin and hungry eyes. Selling balloons. Wiping windshields. Carrying plastic bottles for ten rupees.

Could he be among them now?

Would I even recognise him—if his eyes had turned fearful? If his voice had changed? If someone had given him a new name?

I searched in every place where God was said to exist.

Temples. Mosques. Gurdwaras. Churches.

I didn't care which God.

I just needed *one* of them to be real.

To listen.

To help.

I folded my hands.

Knelt.

Lit diyas, candles, agarbattis.

I placed his photo at the feet of a thousand gods.

I gave up meals.

Gave away money.

Gave everything—

Except hope.

I whispered to the wind, like it might carry my voice into whatever shadow he was trapped in.

"Please… just let him be safe."

But even the wind had nothing to say.

I asked the sky,

"Are you watching this, God?"

"Were you watching when I was sold like scrap?"

"Is this your idea of balance—one stolen boy for another?"

People told me what they always tell the grieving:

"The police are trying."

"Send an email to the child helpline."

"Children go missing every day, bhaiyya."

But he wasn't *a* child.

He was *my* child.

I showed his photo to everyone.

Auto drivers. Cops. Tea vendors. NGO workers.

Some looked with sympathy.

One crumpled the photo without a second thought.

Another said, "It's been too long now."

Too long?

Is that how it works?

Is a child's worth counted in hours… or column inches?

Each night, Rani called.

"Any news?"

And I would hold my breath and lie.

"Maybe tomorrow."

Because how do I say—

"No, Rani, our son is gone and I don't know if I'll ever see him again."

"No, Rani, the world only listens when pain goes viral."

So I lied.

Because courage, sometimes, is just a quiet, daily decision to protect someone else from breaking. Even if you already are.

I met other parents.

At railway platforms. In shelters. Under bridges.

Some had been searching for months.

Some for years.

Some had stopped searching.

They just sat.

Still.

Waiting without waiting.

Like they'd turned into statues carved from grief.

One mother told me she named her missing daughter's doll after her.

Pretending she'd never left.

And I wondered—will that be me someday?

Will I become a ghost of a man, living only in questions?

Even the silence now had a voice.

It screamed in my ears.

Rattled the windows.

Crawled up the walls at night.

I had aged without time passing.

My hands shook.

My eyes burned.

And every heartbeat felt like it was chewing on glass.

Every night, I held the red cap.

Sometimes I swore I could still smell him—

His sweat after play,

The sweet scent of biscuits,

Milk drying on his upper lip.

Every memory stabbed like a needle.

And still—no answers.

Only questions.

Ninety-nine of them.

All written in my mind like unanswered letters to a silent God.

Then came the hundredth:

Will my story end the same way it began—

With a stolen child,

And a broken heart?

Still… I woke up the next morning.

And again the morning after.

Because love doesn't know how to quit.

Even when the world forgets,

Even when the questions outnumber the answers,

Love keeps asking.

Chapter 49 : May be...

Months passed.

Rani stopped sleeping.

I stopped breathing right — not literally, but in every other way that matters.

Dr. Sameer—my father—who once believed medicine could fix anything, now sat at dinner staring into nothing.

Dr. Kavita—my mother—barely spoke — her hands trembled when she stirred her tea.

The house… it wasn't a home anymore.

Just a shell holding memories too loud to ignore.

Akash's laughter still echoed down the hallways, like even the walls missed him.

His toys stayed untouched — frozen in play.

His tiny sandals sat by the door, still facing outward, as if ready to run back in.

But he didn't.

And no matter where I went — market, bus stop, hospital, even a wedding —

I kept searching.

In faces. In voices.

In every little boy's eyes.

But none of them were Akash.

Still… maybe.

Maybe someone took him the same way I was once taken — Like a product. A body with no story.

Maybe he was dragged through cities, sold between shadows, renamed and repurposed.

Maybe right now, he's standing at a red light — barefoot, confused —Holding out a bunch of wilted roses, wiping windshields, blinking against the sun,

Not knowing he once had a mother who hummed lullabies into his neck

And a father who made him giggle just by raising an eyebrow.

Maybe someone told him we left him.

That he wasn't wanted.

That *this* was his fate.

Or maybe —

He's been adopted by a rich, desperate couple.

Maybe he wears branded shoes now. Sleeps on a soft bed with glow-in-the-dark stars above his ceiling.

Maybe they read him bedtime stories…

But none with Rani's tune.

None with *my* voice behind them.

None that tell him he used to love chocolate biscuits and hated brinjals.

Or maybe…

He's far away.

In another country. Another name.

Maybe he speaks a new language — and if I ever heard him, I wouldn't even know it was him.

But still… I believe something.

Something I refuse to let go.

Blood remembers.

A father knows his child.

And a child — no matter where he is, who he becomes — carries the truth in his veins.

Even if they try to scrub it out, rewrite it, bury it under new names and new homes —

That truth is still there.

Beating like a secret drum.

Waiting for a rhythm it once knew — waiting for *me.*

So I don't end this chapter.

Not yet.

Because this story isn't done.

Because Akash's story isn't done.

Some stories don't end —

They wait.

They wait to be found.

To be reclaimed.

And me?

I still walk with hope.

Maybe someday at a railway station.

Maybe in a blurry news article.

Maybe in the tired eyes of a boy who flinches at the sight of a red ribbon…

I'll find him.

And when I do —

I won't ask who told him what.

I won't ask where he's been.

I'll just open my arms and say,
"You took a little longer, beta… but you're home now."

Until then… this page waits.

Not for a full stop —

But for Akash.

Maybe…

And maybe… the next time *you* see a beggar child on the street —

You'll pause.

You'll look again.

You'll wonder, not what he's begging *for,*

But who he's begging *to be remembered by.*

Because sometimes, that boy?

He might be *someone's Akash.*

He might even be *mine.*

Chapter 50 : The Ending Or The Beginning...

I, the author has written every chapter of Deepak's life with love, memory and the fire of a broken heart.

But this chapter… This one, I cannot write.

Because this isn't just Deepak's story anymore.

It's yours too.

You, who read this far.

You, who felt his pain.

You, who maybe have seen a child at a traffic signal and looked away — Or maybe looked too long.

So now, I leave this page blank.

Not because the story is over —

But because the ending… or the beginning… is in *your* hands.

What do *you* think happened to Akash?

Did he find his way back to Deepak & Rani?

Or did he become someone new — somewhere far?

Is he sitting in a classroom right now, trying to remember a lullaby he once heard in a dream?

Or is he standing barefoot in the rain, wondering why no one comes to take him home?

Write it.

Narrate it.

Feel it.

Tell *his* story in your voice.

Because sometimes, the only way to change a broken world…

Is to imagine a better one.

So I'll wait — like this blank page does — for *you.*

And if your heart leads you to it,

share your version of Akash's journey on our last page and on our social page:

written_by_do

Writtenby Do

Maybe your words will light the path he needs.

Maybe your version will become the truth we all needed.

Because who knows?

Maybe… just maybe…

The end of this story

is the beginning of yours.